MY SKY BLUE TRADES

(A sketch of war and after…)

a novel by

Geoff Hastwell

For Dick, with my very best wishes!

24/3/13

Seaview Press

Reprinted 2005, 2006, 2007, 2008, 2009, 2010, 2011, 2012

Printed by:
Salmat Document Management Pty Ltd

National Library of Australia Cataloguing-in-Publication entry
Hastwell, Geoff, 1949- .
 My sky blue trades : a sketch of war and after-- : a novel.
 ISBN 1 74008 324 5.
 1. Australia. Royal Australian Air Force - Fiction. 2.
 World War, 1939-1945 - Fiction. I. Title.
 A823.4

For my father and his friends of 30 Squadron, RAAF.
And for their families…

Through struggle to the stars.
(RAAF credo)

War is not an adventure. It is a disease. It is like
typhus.
(Antoine de Saint-Exupery: 'Flight to Arras')

NEW GUINEA

Madang

PAPUA

Port Mo

CORAL SEA

Cape York

AUST.

BISMARCK SEA

Rabaul

Cape
Hoskins

Cape Gloucester

Talasea

ng

VITIAZ STRAIT

NEW BRITAIN

Jacquinot Bay

Arawe

Gasmata

Lae

HUON
GULF

SOLOMON SEA

Cape Ward Hunt

Kiriwina

Gona

Buna

Goodenough I.

Woodlark I.

Kokoda

Fergusson I.

Port Moresby

Normanby I.

Milne Bay

THANK YOU…

Title *My Sky Blue Trades* and chapter epigraphs taken from
Fern Hill, by Dylan Thomas.
Used with permission of David Higham Associates

Extract from *A Farewell to Arms* by Ernest Hemingway
published by Jonathan Cape.
Used by permission of The Random House Group Limited.

The Servicemen

Len Hastwell, my father and Don West, his navigator, Bob Bennett,
Charles Harris, Doug Raffen, Laurie Crouch, Fred Anderson, Ken
Leonard (all of 30 Squadron) were invaluable sources of anecdotes,
facts, reminiscences and 'good gen'. Keith Collett (22 Squadron)
and Alan Rawlinson (79 Squadron) gave much assistance. Matt
Foley, a coastwatcher I was fortunate to meet in Rabaul, proved a
fount of knowledge and experience. My uncle, Bob Walter, of the
19th Australian Machine Gun Battalion, offered much background
information on the era.

The Civilians

In my Papua New Guinea travel and research, these good friends
provided unstinting support, material and hospitality: Ashley
and Tangala Barnes, Simon Ellis, Enoch and Terrence, Cecilie

Benjamin, Frank Lewis, Peter and Pam Swanson, and the people of Bola Bola on Goodenough Island. (Siaolukaina!)

Mandy Huxtable, Bill Cosgrove's daughter, kindly assisted with information on her father. Cover painting of a Beaufighter is by Adelaide artist, John Boden; cover design is by Qudsia Ahmed. The map of New Guinea and New Britain is by Louise Warren.

To my patient and fastidious editor, Jeanne Mazure, humble thanks!

The Reading

- *Beaufighters Over New Guinea* – George Dick, Royal Australian Airforce Museum, 1993
- *Service in No. 30 Beaufighter Squadron* – George Dick, Adam Press, 1994
- *A Pictorial Record of No. 30 Squadron* – George Dick, self-published
- *Whispering Death* – Neville Parnell, A.H. & A.W. Reed Pty Ltd, 1980
- *Thirty Squadron Operations Log* – Australian War Memorial, Canberra
- *Two Steps to Tokyo* – Gordon Powell, Oxford University press, 1948
- *The Battle of the Bismarck Sea* – Lex McAulay, St Martin's Press, 1991
- *Australia in the War of 1939-1945 – AIR* – Douglas Gillison, Canberra War Memorial, 1962
- *We Were There* – John Barrett, Penguin Books, 1987
- *Wartime – Understanding and Behaviour in the Second World War* – Paul Fussell, Oxford University Press, 1989
- *The War Diaries of Kenneth Slessor* – Ed. Clement Semmler, University of Quld Press, 1985
- *War Diary, 1942* – George Johnston, Collins, 1984

- *Australia's Frontline* – L. Connors, L. Finch, K. Saunders, H. Taylor, University of Qld Press, 1992
- *World War Two* – Ronald Heiferman, Octopus Books, 1973
- *Eyewitness to War – Australia's Pacific Campaign, 1942-1945* – Dreamweaver Magazines
- *Those Ragged, Bloody Heroes* – Peter Brune, Allen and Unwin, 1992
- *Masked Eden – A History of Australians in PNG* –Anne McCosker
- *Beaufighter* – Reginald Kirby, Australasian Publishing Co., 1943
- *Soldiers, An Obituary for Geneva* (a play) – Rolf Hothhuth, Andre Deutsch, 1968
- *Winged Victory* – V.M. Yeates, Jonathan Cape, 1934
- *Whispering Death* – (video) Shane West, Chris Doig
- *The WW Two Films – Damien Parer* (video), Silver Trak Audio and Video.

1

AS I WAS YOUNG AND EASY

"Talk about a ruddy oven!" Ralph Raymond muttered as he swiped yet again at the fly horde besieging him. Around, on three shimmering sides, white swathes of sand and grey green marram grass undulated; to the west the tantalisingly unattainable ocean presented a cool aqua-violet contrast.

He could see little sign in the dunes of the other men from his battery. They had dug in well. He adjusted the large scrubby branch camouflaging their eighteen-pounder and gazed to the northern horizon. "Well, Flinny – how're our chances?" he asked his number two on the gun.

"Reckon they'll have the dickens of a job to winkle us out, Ralph," replied Lance Corporal Ben Flinn. "I can hardly see the blokes on our flanks. We're snug as a bug in a rug."

"And twice as bloody warm! Hope we get the order to load soon. I'm just a bit browned-off with this situation."

Knuckling the ubiquitous sweat from his eyes, Ralph once more squinted to the north. Was that – ? "Get down!" he barked and burrowed back into the boxthorn bush they'd selected for cover and shade.

"They're coming?" asked Flinn, unnecessarily.

"Too right. I saw three – a few thousand feet up."

Then they heard the first faint buzzing, a fluctuating drone in the mid-afternoon. Will the blighters spot us? Ralph wondered, at the same instant wishing he could swap places with one of the men in the aircraft. Fat chance, he thought – what bloody Blue Orchid would toss that in for life down here? He'd have to be barmy!

That morning though, preparing for the army-airforce combined exercise, things seemed straightforward enough. The 49th Militia Battery, 13th Field Brigade gunners had hitched their eighteen-pounders onto light trucks. Re-shod with pneumatic tyres, the guns were easily towed from Woodside Camp and driven at a sedate speed to Adelaide's south coast. Manhandling the weapons through the Moana sandhills hadn't been any picnic, but they'd eventually got them more or less into place. Even satisfied their sergeant. The target drogue, tethered between two barges, had been towed into position and anchored 2,000 yards offshore. Range-finding gear was set up, calculations made, cannon elevation and traverse adjusted accordingly.

Now the militia men just wanted to load, blow the drogue to matchwood and get out of these frying-pan sandhills. Who'd thought of organising the damned stunt in February, anyway …?

Ralph peered up through splinters of thorn as the Ansons came into view overhead. Seemingly the pilots had located their hiding-place – the aircraft began circling directly above. Crikey – if they were enemy kites, and had bombs, Ralph couldn't help thinking.

Half a world away, bombs, shells and bullets *were* being used, with far deadlier intent than mere target practice. Only five months earlier the Germans had gone into Poland, Great Britain declared war and the Commonwealth countries followed suit. Ralph remembered events leading up to the eruption of fighting: tub thumping by Hitler and Mussolini; the useless conferences; constraints and obligations of old and new treaties; promises, betrayals, bluff, counter-bluff and threats. Aspirant empires wanted the same things that old empires possessed. Across Europe, armies, navies and airforces frantically geared up; everywhere, headlines and newsreels trumpeted what people desperately hoped would not be inevitable. Ralph was one of many young Australians taking it in with concern and apprehension and a rising conviction that he had to do his bit in the approaching collision of world forces.

"Heavens above, Dad," he'd stated at an evening meal during the Munich collapse, "the whole Empire's in the firing-line! We can't let Hitler grab whatever he feels like. I'll put in for militia training as soon as I jolly well can!"

"Well, son, you're eighteen years old. It's a big decision, but it's yours to make. I'll stand by you, whichever way you go," replied Mr Raymond steadily.

Ralph's mother was less certain. "Oh Ralph, you *have* weighed this up carefully, I hope?"

"Too right, Mum. I don't want to miss out. There're big things in the wind. I'd like to think I can contribute something."

Beryl, Ralph's thirteen-year-old sister and young brother Alf, just six, were excited and enthusiastic observers of the mealtime discussion. Beryl was mature enough to empathise with both mother and brother's positions; for Alf, the whole thing simply presented a wonderful adventure which he fondly hoped might last long enough for him to enjoy as well.

Not long after that conversation, Ralph joined his local militia unit. Donning khaki, serge, puttees and heavy boots, he began a *lot* of square bashing – but if this was part of the whole box and dice, he felt, so be it. And the militia provided a welcome break from his desk at the Glenelg real-estate company where he'd got his first job.

Today though, even a desk seemed a better proposition than this heat and a million flies and sand-fleas. Then – at last! – the order came to load and fire independently. While the Ansons took it all in from 1,000 feet, the eighteen-pounders were checked, charges rammed home and firing lanyards pulled. But the first shot hit one of the support barges, sent it to the bottom and left the target drogue adrift. Mockingly it wallowed on the light swell. Much chiaking and banter was aimed at the gunners who hadn't aimed so well – and the order followed soon after for the battery to cease firing. Fed up soldiers began to re-limber cannon for the weary return trip to Woodside. The open-site shoot was a fizzer, at least for most of the militia men.

Ralph Raymond however, couldn't forget the aircraft. By Jiminy, he thought, as he and Lance Corporal Flinn readied their gun for its homeward journey, I'd rather be up there doing the looking than down here being looked at. Any day. The notion took root, grew.

Back in Adelaide, the young man made inquiries. He soon discovered that with his Leaving Certificate, he was eligible to apply for RAAF service and did exactly that. The relevant paperwork was quickly completed, a very thorough medical undergone and passed. A few months later Ralph received the telegram ordering him to report to the RAAF Number 4 Initial Training School at Victor Harbor. The airforce had accepted him. It was November 11th, 1940. He would never forget the date. Whatever lay ahead, for better or worse, Ralph Raymond was going to do his utmost to make his war a flying one.

Bill Tassicker was a good footballer. He'd been first ruck of the Richmond Tigers for two seasons, enjoying the responsibility of spearheading his team's attacking game. '*Eat 'em Alive!*' roared the Tigers' war-cry, and Bill – six feet three inches tall and brim-full of life – was the human epitome of that threat. The black and gold flew proudly and often at football ovals around Melbourne when Bill played.

By the end of the '38 winter though, Blind Freddie could see a war coming. Not to be in it was out of the question for Bill, footy or no footy. More difficult was the matter of Ruby, his girl. After one of the last home games that season, Bill broached the issue with her in the Botanic Gardens Café, not far from Richmond Oval.

"I'd like to join up, Rube," he said quietly, stirring his tepid and untasted cup of tea. "Can't see myself staying home when other blokes're doing the right thing …"

Ruby Town, her hazel eyes shining against the pallor of her face, nodded, trying to understand. "Oh, Bill – I know you've been thinking a lot about this. How could you avoid it with all the talk on the wireless and in the papers? But there's no war yet – why do you have to join the army now?"

"Rube, it's not that I want to leave you – far from it, darling. But I reckon I've got to be ready for when the balloon does go up. Hitler's not about to back down – he's been preparing for ages. We're bound to go in soon – next year at the latest, I reckon. And you know I'm not a shirker, Rube."

"No, not at all, Bill. But you might be sent overseas – to England or Germany … I – I'd be worried for you every moment you were gone."

"It'd be the same for me, sweet. The footy can wait, but it's us I'm really thinking about. Maybe the jolly fighting won't last too long …" Bill was more hopeful than certain on that point. Then he reached into his coat pocket, fumbled for a few seconds and withdrew a small maroon box. He placed it on the table before the young woman and levered open the lid.

"Rube – I – I wonder if you'd marry me …? Would you – could you –?"

"Yes, Bill, oh yes! I've been dreaming …" She placed her free hand on Bill's wrist as he lifted the gold band from its box and gently slipped it on her ring finger. He leaned over the small table, clasping Ruby's hands in his and kissed her. Then he sat again, still holding her hands.

"D'you think we can start arrangements straight away, darling?" he asked. "I don't know what's going to happen in the next few months, but I reckon it'll be either army or airforce for me. Navy'd be no good – you know I get seasick on the Yarra!" Bill chuckled. "But the RAAF … that might be the shot – no ruddy marching!"

And they talked of plans for their wedding – the church, guests, members of respective retinues – mixed with snippets of war and peace and where Bill might be sent to fight. So two skeins began unwinding – one towards bliss, the other into unknown darkness; happiness and destruction intertwined.

It was a late spring wedding in welcome sunshine and the Tassicker and Town clans mustered in force. Bill's Uncle Myles and Aunt Vera generously offered the young couple a vacant farmhouse on their Whitfield property for the honeymoon. In the meantime, moving slowly through the military labyrinth, Bill's application for aircrew was travelling to a conclusion.

Back at his Post Office job two months after the wedding the Richmond Tiger received his call-up notice for the RAAF Initial Training School at Somers, Victoria. He was in; it was time to prepare for an approaching war.

With buttock-jarring thumps the Zogling primary glider gained speed across the paddock's grassy surface as its tow-car accelerated. Teeth gritted, Bob kept a fierce grip on the control stick, estimating the best moment to ease back. From the Chev Tourer's open rear seat, straddling the towrope attachment point, his instructor bellowed: *"Now!"* Bob pulled the stick towards his belly, the Zogling lifted and was airborne. After a few moments, his heart racing, the young pilot rotated the controls gently forward to bring his glider banging down onto the grass. For a few more seconds, as the car slowed, the aircraft and its relieved occupant skidded onwards, then slowed to a standstill. One wingtip toppled slowly sideways to rest. The instructor leaped from the car and strolled over to Bob, who grinned broadly as he unbuckled his harness.

"Not bad, Scotty," said the man. "You're picking it up nicely –

didn't get the nose too high at any stage. Want to try a few more skids?"

"My oath!" replied Bob Scott, and began re-connecting his lap strap as the instructor clambered back into the Chev.

So, with some variation in skill of execution, Bob and several other enthusiasts of the Waikerie Gliding Club spent that summer afternoon, bumping and skidding around the hundred-acre paddock on their little Zogling glider. Only as dusk descended did they cease their sport.

Back in the galvanised iron shed which served as hangar, workshop and clubhouse, the aviators relaxed and recapped their day over a few bottles of cold Southwark.

"D'ya reckon Melrose would've stuck this?" joked one of the fliers to the small assembly.

"I dunno," came a rejoinder, "though a fan up front'd sure be an advantage, eh?" The other glider pilots laughingly agreed.

But Jimmy Melrose, doyen of Australia's young aviation heroes was already dead in a flying accident, while the world raced headlong towards war. On his parents' fruitblock near Berri, Bob Scott heard the daily wireless reports and read *The Advertiser's* prognostications. Was it now time to fight – 'to cast away stones', as their old minister had intoned during a Sunday service midway through 1939? For Bob, with his flying skills quite advanced, it seemed as if the airforce would be the best branch of the armed services to join. Besides, it looked like a cleaner way of conducting a war.

So he enlisted in his local RAAF Reserve unit, being accepted only on the rather annoying proviso that he re-enroll in the school he'd left two years previously. However, a determined Bob Scott soon had his mathematics and science up to scratch and was officially 'on the list'. It was almost a year to the day since Menzies' sombre wireless speech announcing his 'melancholy duty' to inform the nation that, with Great Britain's declaration of war on Germany,

'Australia is also at war.' Bob duly received his call-up for active service under the new Empire Air Training Scheme. Britain had just survived the biggest air battle in history; the Germans were, unknown to most, preparing to invade their Russian neighbour; in the north Pacific, Japan extended her cruel grip on Asia. Interesting times, indeed.

In September of 1940, Bob swore the oath 'to serve my country for the duration of the war and for twelve months thereafter,' and boarded a train from Adelaide to Melbourne. Like Bill Tassicker two years earlier he was to begin his RAAF days at Somers.

Ralph Raymond did well in his initial airforce lessons – well enough to move up to Parafield Elementary Flying Training School north of Adelaide. At last he found himself in the cockpit of an aeroplane, not behind some desk or tramping a parade ground.

"All right, Raymond," said Flying Officer Ted Lunn, looking squarely at his pupil. "I want to see you spin this kite by yourself – and hold the jolly thing in for at least three turns, eh!"

"Right you are, sir!" replied the student, hoping he sounded competent and confident. For the young trainee had been more than a little uncomfortable with spins and recovery; the Parafield EFTS instructors knew they would have to rid him of his fear. This flight would be solo – with five solos already under his belt, Ralph was acutely aware how much hung on his performance. He dreaded the thought of being scrubbed and reverting to navigator or air gunner status …

After a good take-off and steady climb Ralph levels off at 5,000 feet and looks groundward. He banks the Gipsy Moth to starboard then to port. Just a bit more height for luck, he thinks, knowing that Lunn will be watching every move he makes – or doesn't make.

Several minutes later, in the cold clear air 8,000 feet above Parafield, Ralph Raymond throttles back and reluctantly accepts that he has no more time to play with. He checks the Sutton harness, pulls his flying goggles hard down over his nose and scrutinizes the sky around and below. All clear – all set. With teeth hard clamped and knees trembling slightly, the pilot throttles off further and eases back on the stick. Obediently the biplane's nose lifts – up, up … It is so still. Then the stall, that terrifying drop. Ralph kicks firmly on the port rudder bar, keeps the stick hard against its rear stop. His Gipsy snaps into the spin, flinging him hard against the cockpit wall. The airfield beneath is a whirling maelstrom of brown and green and grey, air screams through struts and bracing wires. Ralph holds the controls grimly – three, four, five turns, he counts … now – *recover*, a little voice in his head urgently calls. Full right rudder – ease stick forward – equalize rudder – bring her out of dive … Gently, gently … Ralph keeps back-pressure on the stick – and she's coming up – just like the handbook and the instructors said she would. With 'g' forces pumping blood to his head and compressing him into his seat, the pilot jubilantly regains level flight.

"You've done it!" he yells to the world – *"done it!"* And for the next fifteen minutes, to wash off height, puts his Gipsy Moth through every aerobatic manoeuvre he knows: sideslips, steep turns, chandelles … Then down for an above-average landing and taxi to the hangars. Where the broadly grinning Lunn approaches as Ralph, doing his best not to grin, climbs out of the cockpit.

"What did I tell you?" asks the instructor rhetorically. "Congratulations, Raymond – you'll make a pilot yet!"

"I'm glad of that, sir! Can I take her up again to get that recovery sorted out a bit better?"

"Why not? Not that there's much to sort out," Lunn chuckles.

Ruby Tassicker rushed inside with the mail. Settling down in the armchair by the front window she eagerly tore open the envelope and read …

> Royal Australian Airforce,
> No. 2 Service Flying Training School,
> Wagga, NSW,

23rd January, 1941

Dearest Ruby,

How are you, darling? All well I trust, as I hope also for the family. Good to hear the Tigers are looking strong for the next season, but somehow that doesn't seem so important now. Oh for *you* to be here, love! Only thing which helps me stay sane is the flying, and up here at Wagga we're getting plenty of that. The Annie's a dear old bus, slow but reliable. They want us to chalk up hours in them, and in the past fortnight I've flown over 2,000 miles.

Speaking of miles, let me tell you about my trip to Whitfield and Uncle Myles and Aunty Vera's. We were up for some instrument flying, but there was no hood in the kite, so I put it to my number two and a ground staff bloke along for the ride that we do a bit of a cross-country. Of course I wanted to fly up to Whitfield, which is out of our usual area. The other fellows were for it though, so off we went. Didn't have any wind-finding instruments, only a map. Brother, those mountains past Albury are big and *rough!* But you wouldn't believe how pretty the valley looks from the air, Rube. We flew over Beechworth and Myrtleford, then guessed a bit and branched off the narrow gauge line to find Whitfield – a triumph of navigation!

Soon saw Uncle and Aunty's place at the base of the hills on the outskirts of the town. I dived and came down to 200 feet at 180 mph then threw the bus into a climbing turn to avoid the hill. When I pulled up, Wilson, the second pilot, yelled and pointed to his side of the cockpit – the whole starboard window had been dragged away in the pullout! I sent the ground erk back into the turret to see if the tailplane or fin was damaged but luckily they were all right. So then I turned her around and dived again. Aunt Vera was outside by then, waving madly as I came down in the dive. We were just about flat out and I had to be careful to pull up in time. We dived about four times all told and on the last one I did a wingover like a bat out of hell right over the house. Aunt Vera was waving a broom like billy-oh at us. I stood up in the seat and waved back and forgot about the plane for a second. When I sat down again we were doing 200 mph at 100 feet! I gave her full throttle and heaved back on the controls with full aileron and rudder. Didn't take long to get back to 1,000feet and on track for home when I glanced around to the turret door and saw one of the funniest sights ever … It was the poor ground erk – I'd forgotten all about him. The machine-gun slide on the turret had been open and the slipstream must have nearly blown his head off! It was only his second or third flight – reckon I've never seen a bloke looking so *green* as he staggered into the navigator's seat!

But as far as the course goes, you'll be pleased to know I finished tenth overall. The CO complimented us on our performance as the average of marks was the highest they'd had so far. Where we're posted now isn't certain, but I applied for the Middle East when they asked us where we'd like to go. I don't know if that'll make any difference, but that's what I put down. We'll get a week's leave soon and I'll probably know by then.

Keep your chin up, darling. It's one of those things that has to be seen through and finished.

I'm dying to see you again. Write soon!

With All My Love,

Bill

Bill Tassicker did get to the 'Middle East' – the Mediterranean, Abyssinia and Libya. He was assigned to a Bristol Blenheim Squadron, flying this twin-engined heavy fighter against the Italians and giving his all in the fluctuating desert campaign. Many times the accuracy if his rear gunner deterred the CR-32 pilots sufficiently to stave off being shot down, and ground fire – always close – was never close enough to wound the Richmond Tiger.

Royal Australian Airforce,
East Sale,
Victoria,
4th March, 1941

Dear Mum, Dad, Ellie and Betty,

Thanks for your letters and wishes, not to mention the latest Berri news. It all helps me cope with life here at the station.

The RAAF keeps me busy, and the training has it moments, believe me! Over the last few months I've put in hours and hours in Beauforts. They're a decent enough crate, I suppose, though a few have come to grief due to a gremlin we didn't know about in the elevator circuit. The CO eventually grounded 'em all and had our riggers pull one to bits. Found the problem and the kites were soon fixed and back in the air. But Sale got itself a bit of a reputation for a while – new blokes coming in were calling it 'Death Valley', after all the bad news they'd heard about the place!

But yours truly's fit as a fiddle – couldn't be better, so don't go getting yourselves in a tizz about the RAAF. Better than the AIF anyday, I reckon!

Hope the season's going well, Dad, and that you girls are pulling your weight with the picking and pruning and the rest of it. And Mum, I never realised how much I'd miss your cooking till I didn't have it … I'll never take good tucker for granted again, that's for sure!

As for the near future, looks like I'll be here in Aussie for a while longer – you can't get rid of me that easily! Communication and Ferry flying for the moment, which is usually humdrum – unless you run into a spot of rough weather. But it's generally pretty routine, especially compared with the situation in England and Africa, eh? I suppose it all depends on how long the war lasts if I get an overseas posting or not.

Anyway, will keep you informed. Hoping this note finds you all fighting fit.

With Love,

Bob

RAAF
No. 6 Service Flying Training School,
Mallala,
South Australia
14th November, 1941

Dear Mum and Dad,

Sorry I've not written for week or two. The time at Camden was fairly hectic, and we were flat out in the Instructors Course. But the good news is that I got through okay, and am now up to my eyeballs with trainees in Ansons here at Mallala. (Compared with those lovely little Avro Cadets at Camden, they're pretty tame …!)

But mustn't complain – the cockpit of an aeroplane, no matter how slow, still beats foot-slogging any day of the week, in my book.

We had a chuckle at one of our staff pilots a few days ago. They'd called a dispersal exercise, where we had to take a couple of Flights of Ansons to paddocks well out of the aerodrome. After it was completed Sid Boden flew back and complained he'd had trouble trimming his kite – the thing was tail heavy for some reason. When they gave his Anson a close once-over, the riggers fell about laughing. Sid's jolly elevator was filled with wheat heads! He'd obviously torn the fabric on landing or taxiing in the paddock, and unknown to him, had the wheat go into the holes. Lucky he didn't spin once he got airborne!

Of course, the collision you would have read about wasn't so good, was it? We'll never know what actually happened and why they got so close. But eight men killed … Poor devils – we certainly don't want any more, I can tell you.

On a happier note, the world looks beautiful from 10,000 feet, I must say. Not long ago we were up in some light rain, with huge cumulus cloudbanks all around. A rainbow came out, and in the air, you see it as a complete circle … Just corker against the silver white cloud and green-khaki ground below.

Give all my love to Beryl and Alf. I hope their schooling's going well and that Alf is getting the hang of arithmetic. Tell him it'll be handy if he wants to join the RAAF! No doubt about good old Beryl, though – she's well on her way to a scholarship, I'm sure.

One thing I really miss is the lawn and garden at home. Up here it's either dust or mud – by the ton …!

Will sign off now and hit the sack. Up at crack of dawn for more instructing. Write when you have a chance – I look forward to your letters very much.

Love,

Ralph

2

NEW MADE CLOUDS

December, 1941. With swift and terrible decisiveness, Japan landed troops at Kota Bharu in northern Malaya and sank half the American Pacific Fleet at its Hawaiian anchorage. Quickly moving down the Malayan Peninsula, attacking the Philippines and threatening the Dutch East Indies Empire, the Nippon war machine demonstrated graphically just how much it had been underestimated. Singapore fell. Bill's squadron, hastily redeployed from Africa to bases in Sumatra, mounted countless desperate sorties against the new enemy. But the Japanese Army and Navy Airforce machines flew rings around the Blenheim; there were just so many of them – bombers and fighters – and they struck relentlessly. Often caught on the ground, Bill's squadron lost plane after plane. In less than a month only eight of the original twenty-four Blenheims remained operational. Much hasty re-grouping – or, less euphemistically, retreating – occurred.

In March of 1942 the pitiful remnants of the squadron found itself on the south coast of Java, with little fuel, no bombs or machine-gun ammo, non-existent maintenance facilities and Japanese troops landing at beach-heads fearfully close by. A small band of RAF and RAAF personnel assembled on the Tjilatjap dock area as Dutch engineers blew the bridge to the mainland. The airmen were intent on scavenging seaworthy boats in which to escape across the Indian Ocean to Australia. Flight Sergeant Bill Tassicker was with them. A hasty reconnaissance discovered two abandoned 30-foot ship's lifeboats and a crew was quickly assigned to each one. The men loaded supplies of food and water, a sextant, two compasses and a primitive map. They had no charts. Their two small vessels put to sea in heavy weather and while attempting to negotiate a passage past a reef, one boat was holed. Back to shore the weary crews rowed, where they elected to try again in the remaining craft. Bill's luck held – with his fitness little diminished from football days, the young Flight Sergeant proved up to the mark. Eleven men under the command of an English Wingco put to sea once more, even as the town and harbour installations blazed behind them. The men left behind would have to take their chances with the Japanese.

The escape was no milkrun. Their little boat was only a few nautical miles off the coast when a Japanese submarine surfaced close by. The airmen-turned-sailors froze on their thwarts as it closed, an officer on the conning tower surveying them through binoculars while ratings stood by on deck guns. The sub cruised around the boat, only 100 yards away. Then, to the escapees' amazement, the enemy crew disappeared into their vessel and submerged! For some reason the Japanese had spared them – amidst cheers and much shaking of hands, beer was broken out and quaffed in celebration.

Obtaining drinking water would be a major problem. During the frequent rainstorms they collected as much freshwater as possible in a tarpaulin, but the rough weather also meant risk of capsizing. In one particularly heavy squall the rudder came away. Bill, who'd been continually extolling the attributes of the Richmond Tigers, decided to support his words with actions. He was the first to volunteer to go over the side to try to get the vital equipment in working order. Several times he and one or two other men had to tread water while pounding and twisting and cursing at stubborn metal and timber. Eventually the jury-rigged rudder was useable again. They sailed and rowed on.

The sailors had been at sea four weeks when someone yelled: "Christ – look over there!" Two hundred yards astern a whale and its calf broke surface. The mother remained still but her calf swam towards them, intent on investigating this unfamiliar object in its domain. However the young whale was twice the length of their boat, as the awestruck men found when it cruised alongside. Here the calf rested, its mighty flukes beneath their keel and regarded the crew with a calm, inquisitive eye. Each man, scarcely daring to breathe, stared back until the satisfied creature turned and swam back to its mother. More beer was consumed.

Forty days after leaving Java, Bill's company sighted seabirds. A few days later a small island appeared on the horizon. The delighted men made landfall, staggering and collapsing like drunkards at the unfamiliar sensation of solid ground under their feet. As the island was uninhabited, they were soon sailing southwest for the mainland they hoped would not be far ahead.

Suddenly, a drone in the afternoon sky – it was a Catalina recce plane and it had obviously spotted them! Soon after the machine splashed down a few hundred yards away and taxied over. Excited greetings were exchanged and the exhausted but jubilant men left the little craft which had carried them so well. Bill Tassicker was on his way back to Australia, to fly and fight another day. And he hadn't been seasick once!

Even as Bill's weary company made its way from the maw of defeat and captivity, plans were being drawn up in Australia to strike back at the nearby enemy. One new part of the war mosaic began at Richmond RAAF Station out of Sydney. With men from various airforce units and groundstaff from the Aircraft Depot at Richmond, No. 30 Squadron was born. It would be equipped with the Bristol Aircraft Company's Beaufighter and led by Squadron Leader Brian 'Ace' Walters.

The CO made himself as familiar as possible with the flight manual of the anticipated machine. One early June afternoon in the Richmond Airmen's mess, 'Ace' addressed the men who would form the nucleus of 30 Squadron.

"Yes, gentlemen, she's done lot of corker night fighter work in England and by all accounts has given the Jerries and Ities a torrid time in Africa and the Med. The 'Beau' is fast, has a hell of a punch, and is apparently quite manoeuverable for a 10 ton kite. She's got a few vices, mind you. First and foremost getting her on and off the deck … The Hercules XI motors are bloody powerful – 1,560 horsepower – and they build up revs fast. And with both airscrews rotating the same way she can develop a swing to starboard on ground run. The Pom pilots say it's best to bring power up slowly until you have enough airflow over your control surfaces to hold her, then turn on the taps. It seems some fellows lead a bit with the starboard throttle – I'll certainly be looking at all options when we get our first kite. I said the Beau packs a punch and I kid you not one iota! *Four* 20-mil Hispano cannon in the nose, right under the pilot, and six point 303 machine-guns in the wings. They deliver their ammo at the rate of *half a ton per minute* – God help any blighter on the other end of your attack! By the way, the Brits have given our new kite a nice little nickname. With the motors being sleeve valve, she's very quiet in the air – you don't know a Beau is coming till she's shooting you up – and by then it's too late. So the Poms've dubbed her 'Whispering Death'. Naturally we're looking foward to seeing whether or not the Japs agree with the sobriquet!"

The Japanese however, were yet to make their acquaintance with the Beaufighter. Not so far from Australia's northern approaches the Imperial Army and Navy of the Rising Sun appeared unstoppable. The Dutch East Indies Empire which Bill's Blenheims had tried vainly to defend ceased to be run by the Dutch. In February 1942 a huge force of Japanese Kates, Vals and the deadly A6M-Zero-sen plastered Darwin with more bombs than had been dropped on Pearl Harbour. In Papua New Guinea, Lae, Madang, Wewak, Salamaua, Buna and Gona fell to the Japanese. Only the American naval victories at Midway and the Coral Sea provided respite, while at Port Moresby on the southern coast of Papua, defenders held on grimly beneath ton after ton of enemy bombs. To the northeast on the island of New Britain, the enemy consolidated the major base he'd seized at Rabaul. Here the natural volcanic Simpson Harbour provided a perfect springboard for building or extending five airfields, from which the Navy Airforce would operate its bombers and fighters.

Later in June the first Beaufighters, transported from England by merchant ship, arrived in Australia. They were assembled at Laverton then flown up to Richmond for flight training with 30 Squadron. Twenty-four of the new machines were soon on line, and the tricky business of conversion to type began.

"The bright spark who called 'em 'Beaus' sure needs his head read," commented a Flight Sergeant to a fellow 30 Squadron pilot in the Richmond Mess after a day's flying in mid June. They had been working hard getting to know their new aircraft.

"Lord yes – not a pretty beast, is she?" responded the fellow airman. "And funny how the donks stick out *ahead* of the nose. They sure as hell make it hard for lookout to port and starboard, eh?"

"But no doubt about it, she's nippy! After a jolly Beaufort, by Jove, there's not much that'll come close to catching her, in my book. The Nips'd better be on their toes when we get in the war. Mark my words!"

"That's if we ever sort out those ruddy take-offs, eh, Len! Stopping that bloody swing as the revs come up is the tricky bit."

"You're not wrong there, sport! Strewth – I found myself going sideways on the ground run for a moment or two yesterday! Not to mention that twitchy ruddy elevator. With the servos she sure is pitch-sensitive – like taking off on a jolly kangaroo!"

But somehow the new pilots began to master their new mounts. Soon Beaufighters were a familiar sight in the air around Sydney and Richmond as the Squadron gained hours and confidence on them.

In the Richmond workshops, ground crew – fitters, riggers and armourers – made their own acquaintance with this novel aircraft. Its unusual sleeve-valve motors, particularly in comparison with the conventional poppet-valve configuration, offered conundrum loaded with mystery.

"Christ Almighty – what sort of a motor *is* this thing?" commented an exasperated fitter to his fellow in one of the hangars. On the floor sitting solidly on its stand was the Hercules engine they'd been pulling down for the last hour and a half.

"Blimey, mate, I dunno if we'll ever get the hang of this flamin' sleeve valve system. *No* valve stems, *no* springs or tappets. She's a bloody marvel all right!"

"And as for these rotten cam carburettors … Will we ever get the jolly flow worked out good an' proper. Reckon a man needs to be a bloody Rhodes Scholar!"

Luckily the new squadron did not need to go to that extent, as by determined trial and error, the groundstaff eventually had every aeroplane flying well.

The navigators who completed the Beaufighter's crew of two began training on the new AT5/AR8 Australian-designed radio, soon mastering it and maintaining reliable communication with the civilian Aeradio network.

On the 6th August, 1942, a Secret Warning Order was issued by Squadron Leader Walters, alerting his section commanders to prepare for a move. The Squadron winter kit was to be exchanged for tropical active service gear. Where else, the men reasoned, than to New Guinea? With everyone only too well clued up on Japanese moves on the Kokoda Track, it was their obvious destination.

Soon 300 groundstaff under the command of several pilot officers marched to Clarendon Railway Station, led by an RAAF band playing 'Ace's' oft-sung ditty, *We're a Bunch of Bastards* and *Off We Go to Meet the Savage Foe.* Their long train journey took them to Queensland, where they disembarked at Bohle River, near Townsville. Late in August 24 Beaufighters, each carrying two extra men besides pilot and navigator, flew up to join them.

Awaiting further orders, the Beaufighter crews began training hard for whatever tasks awaited them in New Guinea. The emphasis was on map-reading and low flying over the mountainous terrain of coastal Queensland. They often accompanied Douglas A-20 Boston Bombers of 22 Squadron, also destined for New Guinea and quickly developed effective tactics for combined ops.

In early September the groundstaff embarked on the *SS Taroona* while stores were loaded on the *Bontekoe Batavia*. With the escort frigate *HMAS Swan* they sailed for Port Moresby.

A few days later the Beaufighters departed Garbutt Strip at Townsville, touching down at Moresby after an uneventful three and a half hour crossing of the Coral Sea. A campsite had already been cleared and established among kunai grass and eucalypts just over two miles from their operational airfield, simply known as Ward's Strip. Thirty Squadron was ready for war.

3

CHILDREN GREEN AND GOLDEN

Of our three airmen, Bob Scott was the first to join the new Squadron. In late 1941 he had been posted to the General Reconnaissance School at Laverton as a Staff Pilot. Here he helped train navigators. It meant a lot of flying through all sorts of weather out over Bass Strait, usually in Ansons. With winds shifting considerably once they cleared the Port Phillip Bay Heads, the poor navs often found their calculations hopelessly out. Bob would usually oblige with a hint or two on best track and heading.

Then came the day that Flying Officer Scott ferried an Anson to the Station at Cressy and saw a Beaufighter land. Immediately struck by the power and speed of the unfamiliar aircraft, he asked who'd brought it in. When Bob discovered its pilot was none other than Squadron Leader Walters himself, he made up his mind. That evening Bob approached 'Ace' in the Mess. "Sir," he said, "that aircraft of yours is just magnificent – I'd give my right arm to fly one on ops. What's the chance of a spot in your Squadron?"

"We're always on the lookout for good aircrew," replied the CO. "Reckon you can fit the bill?"

"I know I can, sir," said Bob.

"All right Scott, I'll see what I can do."

Walters was true to his word. A month later Bob Scott received his transfer to No. 1 Course, 5 Operational Training Unit at Wagga. Initiation for entrance to 30 Squadron meant flying dual in the aircraft from which much of the Beaufighter had been derived – the Beaufort light bomber. Bob had not forgotten his experience in Beauforts at Sale, but still viewed his transition to a Beaufighter with some anxiety. White-faced fellow pilots had told him of the Beau's tendency to swing on take-off and how difficult it was to establish a horizon without a nose reference in front of the cockpit. But Bob's first solo in the new aircraft, in September of '42, went smoothly. "I led a bit with starboard throttle on ground run and just eased on the taps," he said afterwards. "She behaved beautifully – straight as an arrow. And when she came in on final, I just held off until those great big wheels went 'grrr – plonk', and she was on the deck. Almost a piece of cake!"

Bob's second flight in the Beaufighter was anything *but* a piece of cake. Once again flying without a navigator (the RAAF reasoning pragmatically that it was cheaper to lose one airman than two in the event of a prang), Bob took off confidently. Strange how much longer she took to leave the ground than the previous day, though wind strength was about the same. Then, in the air, the Beau handled sluggishly and heavily, a stark contrast to the nimble machine of yesterday. Like a bloody sack of cement, thought Bob – she's just not penetrating! He decided to cut short his flight and land the aircraft before anything else popped up out of the blue. He lowered the undercarriage and sure enough, there *was* another thing. On checking that his undercart was locked in position, Bob was horrified to see that the port wheel had lost its tyre – probably a blowout on take-off. What was left of the mangled rubber hung on the axle, flapping madly in the airflow. Good Lord, he thought, how am I going to get this crate down without a ground loop or writing off a ruddy wing?

There is nothing to do but burn off fuel in the airfield locality and inform the tower of his predicament. With every nerve in his body jumping, mouth bone dry and jaws clamped tight, Bob joins circuit and eases the Beaufighter gently onto final approach – as gently as the heavily handling machine allows. Throttle back; flaps set; speed 120 knots and trimmed. Bob clears the near fence and floats down the field, as ready as he can be for the first touch of wheel on grass. He braces himself to keep controls to starboard, and ready with opposite rudder to counteract yaw, desperately hopes his port wing will stay up for as long as possible. BUMP! Down and rolling, fast, on the starboard wheel. Ease on wheel brake. Keep controls hard over – she's losing speed, rolling. Port wheel and that useless tyre still off the deck … CRACK! Port wheel now down, and chewing into the grass … She's turning – hold rudder over … Coming straight – straightening – keep her on track …. Slowing, with no ground loop, no wing collapse … Stopped – and okay! Bob releases a long, grateful sigh and with shaking hands switches off and undoes his harness. Groggily, carefully, jubilantly, the young pilot makes his way from his aircraft via the belly ladder in the well behind his seat. He stares incredulously at the port wheel, from which hangs the parody of a tyre. The naked rim shows no damage apart from a little burring on its edge. A fitter strolls across from the nearest hangar.

"Jeez – your luck's in today, mate," he offers. "A one-wheel landing, and look at your nav blister!"

Bob steps out from under the wing and immediately spots the reason why his plane has handled so poorly: the navigator's canopy and fairing are dangling, open, on their hinges. *That* has been the cause of all the drag and terrible aerodynamics of the Beaufighter.

"I'm damned lucky the thing didn't come off and wipe out my tail, eh, Stan?" Bob comments to the fitter. "Let's call it a day – I could do with a wee pick-me-up!"

And so, in the following weeks, Flying Officer Scott continued training in the 'Whispering Death': low level work; cross-countrys, now with a navigator; air to ground gunnery; formation and night-flying. With every hour accrued his skills sharpened and confidence grew. The Beau certainly was a wonderful aeroplane to fly.

After three months at the O.T.U. it was time for an operational posting. Bob would go to join 30 Squadron at Port Moresby. Together with his navigator Flight Sergeant Phil Edmonds, he picked up tropical kit from Stores. Then, having obtained a lift from the always-obliging Yanks, they took off for New Guinea in a C-47.

As they joined circuit for their landing strip Bob observed the general lay-out of Moresby: the crowded harbour with big warehouses along its wharves; rusty remnants of the derelict freighter *Pruth* on her reef in the blue-green bay; low, almost bare hillocks with dense bright green rainforest patches in their fissures; tents by the hundred; supply dumps; vehicles making their dusty way along connecting tracks; distant smoke – probably from local natives burning off scrub for their gardens. Inland to the north, the 13,000-foot peaks of the Owen Stanley mountain range provided a spectacular backdrop.

"Well, Phil, we're in the war!" Bob commented to his navigator on the webbing seat beside him.

"Dit dit dit, dah dah dah, dit dit dit," grunted Phil, who often relied on Morse to communicate. In this instance, he simply and eloquently spelled 'S.O.S.'

Soon after landing, having slung their gear into a jeep (the Yanks seemed to have no shortage of equipment), Bob and Phil were driven to the Australian camp two miles away. The track wound through low scrub and gum trees, so familiar to Bob from the Riverland paddocks of home. Finally, the road opened into a large clearing. This was bordered by dozens of tents and a few tin buildings of utilitarian appearance. A dilapidated roughly lettered sign hanging from a tree informed the new arrivals that they were in 'Goon Valley'.

As their driver roared off to an accompaniment of crunching

gears and a cheerful, "So long, buddies," the two airmen noticed a tall khaki-clad figure approaching. He wore the RAAF navy peaked officer's cap, a well-washed long-sleeved shirt with epaulettes, trousers, gaiters and shiny black boots. Almost marching across the clearing, the officer stepped out precisely, swinging arms in a soldierly parade ground manner. He halted in front of them and paused expectantly. At the same moment Bob and Phil guessed that he was waiting for a salute; the new arrivals hurriedly came to attention and flung hands up to their caps.

"At ease, gentlemen," the officer barked, saluting crisply. "Welcome to 30 Squadron. I am Flight Lieutenant Warnes, Squadron Adjutant. I take it that you are Flying Officer Robert Scott and Flight Sergeant Phillip Edmonds. Is that correct?"

"Er – yes sir," replied Bob.

"Good. We've been expecting you. Nice to have a few new crew on board – things've been hotting up lately."

The new chums couldn't help glancing at each other, as Adjutant Warnes continued. "Come with me – bring your equipment – and we'll see about a tent. I'll introduce you to your Flight Leader. We'll catch up with the CO later."

So Bob and his 'oppo' came to 30 Squadron. Warnes allocated them a tent in a group scattered amongst the kunai and eucalypts, then took them over to the Mess. This was the largest tent in the camp, an impressive marquee supported by several vertical poles and constructed of thick khaki canvas. The three men ducked under its door flap to find themselves in a shadier but only marginally cooler mess area. Bob and Phil took in several long trestle tables and benches and a sparsely equipped bar to one side. There seemed to be minimal – if any – alcohol available, Bob observed.

"Maybe Blamey was right about no grog in New Guinea, eh, Phil?" he grunted to his companion.

"You're not wrong, cobber!" replied Phil

But now two of the Squadron airmen were approaching from

the half dozen or so men in the Mess. Warnes saw them nearing and said: "I'll leave you in good hands, gentlemen. Afraid the CO wants some paperwork completed post-haste, and that's my little job. I'll see you at dinnertime. If you have any questions, don't hesitate to ask. Good day."

Warnes turned smartly on his heel and marched out of the Mess tent. A ruddy-faced Flight Lieutenant grinned at them and offered his hand.

"Gidday – my name's Ross Small. Don't worry about 'Splitpin' – he eats RAAF manuals for morning tea, poor old bugger. But underneath he's the salt of the earth – without 'im, 'Ace'd' be snowed under with bumph. Speaking of 'Ace', the CO'll probably want us to get together with you blokes pretty soon for a bit of a conflab on operational set-up, then organise a familiarisation flight or two. You fellows're down for 'A' Flight, and I'm the blighter in charge."

"Ta for that, Ross. But why's the Adjutant called 'Splitpin'?" asked Bob.

"Just wait till he takes off his cap, mate – wait till he takes off his cap!" chortled Ross.

"You need to show more respect for your superiors, Flight Lieutenant," grinned a short brown-skinned man alongside Small. "Gidday – me name's Tom Arthur. I help run 'Grumpy's Joint' – that is, when I'm not bein' chucked around in the back of Ross's kite over some ack-ack ridden Jap target on the north coast."

" 'Grumpy' Edgerton's the leader of 'B' Flight. He also oversees bar amenities for the Squadron. The 'Joint' – such as it is – is in his tender care," offered Ross. "By the way, do either of you blokes play table-tennis? We're looking to knock Bob Bennett off the top of the ladder and to date nobody's up to the task."

"I'm no threat," said Phil. "How about you, Bob?"

"Played a bit in my old youth club at Berri," replied the pilot. "Seems a hundred years ago now, though."

"We'll have to organise a tournament," promised Ross. "Mind you, no-one's able to touch the ruddy Yanks at baseball! You can hardly see their pitches let alone hit the bloody thing. Those blokes can *really* chuck a ball!"

"But we'll sign you up for footy," said Tom. "The 22 Squadron bludgers think they're somethin', but given half a chance we'll have 'em on toast. You would've played a bit in Aussie wouldn't ya?" he asked hopefully.

"Just mucking around in the local paddocks," said Bob. "But you wouldn't think there was a war on, with all this sport on offer!"

"Ah, don't get us wrong, cobber," said Ross. "You'll have more than enough chances at the Nips, believe me. And the bastards give as good as they get. Stooging about here between rain showers and sorties is one of the few things that keeps us from going troppo!"

"That's where the Kokoda Track starts," yelled Flight Lieutenant Small above the thrum of the Hercules motors. Bob, standing in the well behind Small, observed the Owen Stanley's steep jungle-covered lower slopes and felt a sudden pang for the army men struggling up and down those towering ridges.

"Can you see Kila Strip near the coast and the three airfields inland? We'll mark 'em more clearly on your chart when we get down," said Small. "For now, I'll take us over the old Hood Point Strip for a mock attack, then go home."

And that was the local area familiarisation for Bob and Phil. The new pilot and navigator absorbed a lot over the next few days, going up without a guide soon after. They strafed the *Pruth* wreck in Moresby Harbour, making several high-speed passes at its rusting hulk. Bob saw with satisfaction his cannon and machine-gun rounds slamming into the superstructure before he pulled up and away in the high 'g' climb.

Then they were in at the deep end. A week after the practice strafe on the wreck Bob and Phil saw their names on the Ops Board. It was to be a strike on Madang-Alexishaven, the Japanese bases on the far coast almost due north of Moresby. 'A' Flight was to accompany B-25 bombers and P-40 top cover, both from American Army Airforce squadrons. They would leave at first light the next day. Bob and Phil were to fly number two with Ross Small, their Flight Leader.

Marshalling and take-offs from Ward's go smoothly – no engine malfunctions or other problems – and rendezvous is made on schedule with the Yank Mitchells and Kittyhawks. Then a two-hour hop in formation over two mountain ranges – the Owen Stanleys and the Finisterres. All that jungle! If they are forced down here, assuming by some miracle they find a flat piece of terrain, what chance is there of making it back?

But their ever-reliable motors keep turning and after climbing the second range, the Allied machines swoop low for their strike on the enemy coastal garrison. Approaching the sea they spot a light freighter in the harbour; Small's curt order crackles on their radio at the same instant.

"Get the ship, then the docks. Scotty – stay on my tail!"

And Small increases the angle of his dive, opening throttle. Bob follows him, a few hundred yards behind and to one side of his Leader. Now dozens of little black puffs, like soundlessly fragmenting mushrooms, appear in the air around. It is Bob and Phil's first experience of anti-aircraft fire, and it all seems concentrated on *their* kite! Bob kicks port and starboard rudder pedals, jinking his plane to left and right. Ahead, Small is doing the same. More black puffballs, but now the attackers are almost at sea level, closing on the ship. It looks bow-high in the water – then Bob realises it has been run aground on a shoal. Small fires his first burst. Still slightly abeam and behind, Bob sees the plumes of spray leap high as his Flight Leader opens up. He's long since flicked off 'safety' on the firing-button. Now, with Small pulling up and banking, Bob holds the ship in his reflector sight. He presses the button – frantic hammering of cannons and machine-guns echoes around the cockpit, which fills with cordite fumes. Then he ceases fire, pulls up and over the vessel and rolls to port as Small has done. Phil is shouting on the intercom: "She's caught fire, Bob! I can see Nips jumping off. Well done, mate! Dit dit dit!" Keeping the turn on as they climb, Bob finds a second or two to register the B-25s' bombs hitting the shore installations – wharves and sheds and supply dumps. Higher up, the Kittyhawks are all over the sky, taking on the Japanese fighters which have got airborne. It is a melee of machines, ack-ack and explosions.

"Break off. Break off. We're going home!" radios Small. "Good job, boys!"

And the 30 Squadron aircraft fly inland, forming up with various Mitchells and Kittyhawks.

Debriefing at Ward's several hours later confirmed the extent of their sortie's success. The Japanese dockside buildings and supply dumps had taken quite a bit of damage and the ship was probably accounted for. Best of all every Beau got back, though several bore marks of ack-ack shell burst damage or holes from small arms fire.

Bob and Phil celebrated their first strike by joining a trip to the Rouna Falls, southeast of Goon Valley on the Laloki River. It was here, paddling and splashing in the cool water of the pool below the falls that they discovered the correct name of their campsite.

"Crikey, you silly half-hours – it's *June* Valley, not *Goon* Valley," chortled one of the swimmers when Bob commented on the name. "Ya can't believe every sign ya read around the place. If they were dinky-di we'd be chock-a-block with Yank food and equipment, not to mention five star hotel accommodation!"

"But don't forget the sheilas, mate. I hope they're gonna be real!" cut in another swimmer. "It's high time those nurses hit the island. 'Splitty' reckons they're due any day now."

Not having seen a white woman for several months the 30

Squadron men were naturally impatient for 'Splitpin's' prediction to be made good.

"Trouble is," continued the airman, "'Splitty'll' be down on fraternisation like a ton of bricks!"

"That won't worry 'Casanova' Collins, though – reckons 'e's God's gift to women, never mind what colour!" put in another of the group.

"Do you see many of the local people?" asked Phil.

"A few come in from Hanaubada Village to work with ANGAU and it's all right to trade with 'em. You can get some nice fruit 'n veg sometimes. That's a bloody big improvement on bully-beef and powdered eggs, believe me!"

"Too right," said Bob, nodding vehemently. "That bully's as hard as leather. As for herrings in sauce …!"

"Those bloody goldfish! Vertical or horizontal, they're equally foul," commented their companion. "'Bout bloody time we teed up another pinnace trip to Fisherman's Island with some 'gelly'. Nothin' like fresh seafood, eh?" And he drummed his lean stomach in sharp and appeciative memory. So the swimming-party splashed away the afternoon. Bob and Phil couldn't help feeling that at last they were settling into the Squadron.

Parade next morning was much less congenial. Flight Lieutenant Warnes, fully exhortatory, addressed the Squadron. Each man stood at ease in rank and file, wearing webbing, uniform and tin helmet.

"Yes," the Adjutant boomed, "you may all think Tojo has been a little quiet of late. Well, gentlemen, let me disabuse you on this. We are reliably informed that a big raid is very much in the offing and it could be accompanied by more than bombs. In short, if the Nips come back down the Track they may feel encouraged to deploy paratroops on Moresby itself. My standing orders of last month are therefore to be carried out to the letter by *all* personnel. Groundstaff will have rifles and tin helmets with them at all times while on duty. Aircrews are to store their small-arms and the sub-machine gun in their aircraft. Do not – I repeat – *do not* use these for taking pot-shots at flying-foxes or for larking about in the kunai. Your weapons may well be required for more serious work at very short notice. Slit trenches are to be dug alongside *every* tent, and kept clear of insects and rubbish. And when the air-raid alarm goes up you are to take *immediate* cover. Yes, I am aware that some of you like to observe all the action – for example, tracer – from various vantage-points. This is to cease forthwith. Even our own falling anti-aircraft shrapnel can be dangerous as a few of you are only too well aware! I repeat, gentlemen – you are to be on maximum alert at all times for enemy incursions around the Moresby sector, in particular the strip and camp areas. Very well, parade will come to order … *Atten-shun!* At ease. Parade dismissed.”

It wasn’t quite so easy to dismiss the rumours that Splitpin’s harangue had set loose around the camp.

“Je-he-sus,” said Cliff Clothier at the two-up school behind the Mess tents. “What’s ‘Splitty’ up to? Anyone’d think ’e’d got the wind up, well and truly!”

“Ah, fair go, Clothy,” countered one of school. “He’s only acting on the gen from recco and the coastwatchers. “’Ow’d ya like it if the Nips came over like last time? You know they do just about what they like on their night jobs.”

“An’ ruddy droppin’ paratroops …! Hell’s bells – it’ll be on for young an’ old, eh?” commented another member of the school. The game continued, opinions and pennies rising and falling simultaneously.

In the June Valley kitchen preparing the midday kai, Lola and Brenda were in deep colloquy, their be-scarved heads bent low over pots of powdered potatoes …

“Heavens above!” lamented Lola to his partner, “things could get really nasty. Imagine if those Japanese monsters got here! Why, we’d be slaughtered in our stretchers – *slaughtered …*” Lola was getting close to the teary stage.

"Now, now, dearie,' comforted Brenda, "you know as well as I do that they'd first have to tackle our Army boys – and that just might prove a wee bit of a tall order! And just how much have our Beaus stopped their attacks lately, eh? Seems to me they're keeping up their end of the war very well – not to mention all the Americans! I don't think there's *any* likelihood of those horrible little yellow creatures coming within *coo-ee* of us … No fear!"

And Brenda placed a soothing arm around the slumped shoulders of Lola, who responded with a wan smile.

"Ta – you always know to cheer a fellow up! Let's get on with lunch, eh, ducks?" Which the Squadron cooks set about immediately, with rapidly returning morale.

4

AND THEN TO AWAKE

"Garbutt certainly is a huge airfield. The Yanks don't do things by halves," Ralph Raymond commented to himself as he walked from the tarmac to the Mess on a muggy but clear November afternoon. "Now, if I can just get a good cup of tea, I'll be right," he added. The trip up to Townsville from Laverton had been a shemozzle. Brass hats jumped the queue there and Ralph had to hang around for days waiting for another spare plane seat going north. Then that bloody dose of dysentery! Not much fun before joining your first operational squadron … And he was very much looking forward to that. He'd heard a lot of good news about the Beaufighter boys in New Guinea and he was keen to join them. The O.T.U. at Wagga had provided solid preparation for the war in the tropics; now Ralph wanted to contribute his bit against the Japanese. Never mind the ruddy atebrin tablets. They turned your skin yellow but kept malaria at bay – at least that's what the Laverton MO promised.

Ralph surveyed the large and well-appointed Garbutt Field Officers' Mess. A few tables were occupied by USAAF types in khaki or olive drab, all very crisp and spruced up. Several big ceiling fans moved warm air around the room in lazy swirls. At the bar, a tall man in RAAF uniform was in heated discussion with the orderly.

"Good God, mate – no scotch? You blokes are supposed to've cornered the market for grog in the entire South West Pacific!"

"Yessir, that may be the case, sir," responded the barman patiently, "but we do have fine bourbon, if that's okay."

"No it's *not* okay!" the Australian answered. "I've been bouncin' around in a C-47 for a day and a half and I need the real McCoy to wash away the dust."

Ralph began to take an interest in the conversation. Was this fellow flier heading for New Guinea too? Ralph crossed to the bar and stood beside the other RAAF man.

"Gidday. How are you?" Ralph asked.

"Oh, gidday, mate!" said the tall scotch-seeker, turning to Ralph. "Another Aussie. Hope you're not after a real drink, sport. These coves can't oblige!"

"No, that's not a problem," laughed Ralph. "Just coming off a bout of the runs. Got to be a bit careful what I'm imbibing."

"That's no good – no good at all. By the way, the name's Bill – Bill Tassicker." He offered his hefty hand. Ralph shook it.

"Pleased to meet you. I'm Ralph Raymond. Are you going to the Island?"

"Too right! Up to Moresby with 30 Squadron. Lookin' forward to it."

"How about that," said Ralph delightedly. "So'm I. Went through 5 O.T.U. What d'you think of the Beau?"

"What do I think?" Bill launched into an enthusiastic account of his Beaufighter experience, contrasting his new mount with the old Blenheim, much to the latter's detriment. Briefly he related his anxious time in Java and the boat journey to Australia.

"Some jaunt!" Ralph said with a sharp whistle. "Now you'll be returning the favour, eh? Bet you're keen as mustard on that score."

"You're not wrong! But the wife's expecting. I just hope I'll be in Melbourne when the little one arrives …" Bill gazed straight ahead, forgetting his need for a drink. Ruby and their unborn baby were too far away, yet – for a few moments – overwhelmingly near. Ralph had known plenty of girls in Adelaide but none had been more than casual flings in the shallow social stream of those days. He could nevertheless understand Bill's ache, the yearning for life to be complete.

"It'll come up trumps, don't you worry. A six-month tour of ops and in Beaus – not bloody Hudsons or Beauforts. We'll be right as rain, Bill. You'll be back in Aussie before you know it!"

"Out with the boys on Richmond Oval – that'll be just the shot, cobber!" said Bill, punching his companion lightly on the shoulder. "Can't wait to be ruckin' again with the Tigers. Jack Dyer's promised us a flag and by Jeez I'd love to be in the side that wins it!"

The tenor of their chat remained jovial and Ralph even obtained a cup of passable tea. Bill had to settle for bourbon but found it more than acceptable. They discovered that a flying boat would be leaving Townsville Harbour the next morning and inquiries indicated room aboard for two more. Ralph and Bill slept soundly that night in the Officers' Quarters. Across the Coral Sea, the dark jungle and cumulus-filled skies of New Guinea awaited.

The new pilots quickly found places in the Squadron. Like Bob and Phil they were provided with tents and stretchers, flew the familiarisation flights around Moresby and down to Milne Bay and generally prepared for the war they had signed into. From the pool of new WAGS they selected and got to know an 'oppo' – the man who would navigate, load the cannon and be the Beau's rear 'eyes' in action.

Ralph made friends with Don Eastway, a stocky navigator from Newcastle and rapidly came to like Don's no-fuss, low key and gently sardonic approach to Squadron life. Bill teamed up with

Bernie Griffiths who'd been a maths teacher in Perth in pre-war days. Gradually the new crews came to know their machines and each other. The three – aeroplane, pilot and navigator – would need to form a close and interdependent unit if they were to see the war through.

'Ace' wanted to get new men into things quickly while they were still fresh and relatively keen to come to grips with the opposition. The CO well knew, as did every old hand, just how soon the tropics and the casualty rate blunted bellicose appetites. And who better than 'Ace' to appreciate just what the Japanese could dish up? He'd already had one spectacular wheels-up landing when his hydraulics had been shot out over Lae. Another time an ack-ack shell had pierced the fuselage just forward of his navigator, without – thank God – exploding. It was a war no shiny-bum, no matter how many communiqués he read or wrote, could ever really understand.

Two weeks before Christmas of 1942, plans were being finalised for a strike on the Salamaua Isthmus. This was an enemy strongpoint on the north coast just below Lae and the Japanese defended it heavily. As the Beaufighters were usually low down, ground strafing, the risk of copping one increased.

Ross Small spoke with understandable energy on the topic to Bob, Ralph and Bill in the Mess after their evening kai. "Oh yeah – the Yanks reckon we're barmy," he said. The men paused in their game of Slippery Sam as the Flight Lieutenant elaborated on his premise. "The Mitchell and Fortress blokes are up at 8,000 to 10,000 feet. We're at *100* feet and *lower!* Apart from the fact that the Yanks sometimes get rid of their ordnance too early, bang on top of us, we've got to fly right into everything the Nips're putting up. They *know* we're coming in low so most of their ack-ack is fused to go off at a few hundred feet. Not to mention the small arms stuff – they've got heavy machine-guns, automatic weapons, the works – all goin' bananas … Even a rifle bullet can cut an air or fuel line. Not much fun."

"What do you do about fighters?" asked Ralph with trepidation. "I've heard they're pretty good."

"You heard right! They know their onions, especially the Navy pilots. Those buggers fly bloody well and they're not afraid to mix it. The Lightning and Kittyhawk boys have their hands full when the Jap gets wind of one of our strikes and has kites in the air. Do they ever *move!* We don't have any show of dog-fightin' 'em, no matter what you read down south and all the Kittyhawk coves can do is dive, shoot and climb away. You'll never turn inside a Zero and you'll never out-manoeuvre 'im. As far as the Beau goes, if a fighter makes an attack on you, bank towards 'im and head for the deck, flat out. At sea level, if 'e's managed to get on your tail, he usually can't close – thank your lucky stars for those beautiful Hercs – when they get a full steam up, they *go*, no mistake. Without a rear gun, our oppos sometimes flash the Aldis lamp to make the Jap think we're shootin' back. But the best thing your navs can do is to tell you when to jink port or starboard. Done properly, this'll throw the Nip off his aim. And on the deck it'll blow up spray and turbulence so he can't get a steady firing platform. After twenty minutes or so, the bandit'll usually pull up and break off. I've even see 'em give a wing-waggle as if to say: 'See ya – till next time …' But God help you if you lose a motor. The Jap'll eat you for breakfast then unless you're lucky enough to have top cover to nurse-maid you back home."

"So, Salamaua, here we come," said Bill cheerfully. "Hey, Bernie, what say we wander down to dispersal and see how my little job's coming along?"

"Sure thing, Tassie," replied Bernie. They pushed back their chairs and headed out of the Mess tent with a "Cheerio".

"What's the 'job', Ross?" asked Ralph.

"Oh, Bill's going to give the same message to the Jap that he gave the Ities. Apparently, over in Africa he had a tiger's head painted on the nose of his Blenheim, plus the Richmond footy war cry: *'Eat 'em Alive'*. And knowin' Bill, he jolly well means it, too!" Ross was well aware of how keen Bill Tassicker was to get back in the fight.

The Slippery Sam continued in a desultory fashion as the ping-pong aficionados energetically patted celluloid back and forth across their table and groups of airmen played cards, smoked and yarned at tables around the Mess. One thing about 'Ace' – his insistence on a common Mess for all ranks did wonders for morale, allowing pilots and navigators to socialize off-duty. It had quickly got rid of that rigid military division between officers and NCOs engendered by separate Messes.

But the Salamaua op waited. It was to be a 'B' Flight affair with six aircraft led by 'Blazer' Wren, the red-topped Flight Lieutenant well known in the Squadron for a temper as fiery as his follicles. Both Ralph and Bill were listed on the Ops Board. Take-off was down for 0600 hours. All going well, this would give them an ETA at Salamaua out of the sun, taking the Japanese by surprise.

Later that night under the glare of their hissing Colemans, pilots and navigators discussed the morning to come. Ralph told Don he liked Ross Small's advice in the event of being jumped.

"Heavens, yes," replied the navigator, "get away as quick as we can. But if we were hit – by ack-ack, if not by a fighter – what's the best plan, Ralph?"

"I've been going over it, Don, believe me. Not much chance to bale out at the height we'd have. Reckon our best bet'd be to head out to sea and try ditching. You'd want to get a fast signal off with co-ordinates to give search and rescue a show of finding us. They say a Beau'll float for about thirty seconds if you get her down all right …"

"Hoo-ee! We'd need to be out quick as a flash, eh, Ralph?"

"Too right. And then hope the dinghy'll inflate and that the Japs wouldn't have too many boats in the area."

"It doesn't bear thinking about if we got captured. Bob

recommends tellin' 'em anything – be as co-operative as all hell. If they send you to a rear area like Rabaul, you'll stand more of a chance, he reckons."

"Bob could have a point, Don. I know the Nips in New Guinea hate our guts because of the strife we've given 'em on the Kokoda Track and other places. But to work you over with bayonets … Not too flash, is it?"

Similar sombre thoughts were being shared by Bill and Bernie in their tent not far away. "But by God, Bernie," said Bill, "I wouldn't go down without taking one or two of the bastards with me!" He patted the .38 revolver in its webbing on the rough bench by his stretcher.

"Christ, Bill, they'd go us worse than ever then! Not much chop either way, in my book!"

"Well, let's cross that bridge when we have to, mate. Till then I'm going to take our kite right in an' give the Nips the works. Hey, Al and Murray did a beaut job on our tiger, eh?"

"My oath – it looks terrific. Jack Dyer'd be proud of you, Bill!"

Then came the scuff of approaching footsteps and they heard a cheerful, unfamiliar voice outside. "Hello – anybody home?"

"Friend or foe?" joked Bill. "But come in anyway – less mozzies in here."

The tent flap lifted and a slim, sallow figure clad in long-sleeved khaki shirt and trousers ducked in.

"Good evening, men," he said. "I'm Padre Kirk. Just popping around to get to know our new arrivals."

"Pleased to meet you, Padre," replied Bill. He introduced himself and Bernie, and they cleared a space on one of the boxes to make a seat for their visitor. Soon, over a mug of 'choofer' heated tea, the padre was in full flight.

"It certainly is an exciting time to be in New Guinea," he enthused. "All the gen points to a real turning of the tide. And it's splendid young chaps like yourselves who're responsible!" The chaplain beamed and produced a notebook and pencil. "I wonder if you'd be good enough to oblige me with a few first impressions of the Squadron. I'm gathering bits and pieces for a book I'm working on about this part of the War. A little boost for the people on our Home Front, you might say …" For the next three quarters of an hour, Padre Kirk plied Bill and Bernie with queries about their training, previous experience (the minister was fascinated by Bill's boat adventures), opinions of June Valley, what a Beau was like to fly and many other questions. Bill and Bernie were pleased to help, but each man gained the uncomfortable feeling that he was being 'grilled' – almost as if by an enemy interrogator.

Then snapping shut his notebook and taking a final sip of tea, the padre rose. "Thanks very much, fellows," he said. "You've been a great help. I'd better let you get some shut-eye now though, with that op tomorrow. Safe flying, straight shooting, eh? We'll see you back in no time. Good evening." He solemnly shook hands, stepped under the door flap and was gone.

"Jumpin' Jehosaphat!" said Bernie. "The old padre sure does turn it on, eh?"

"You're not wrong there, mate," replied Bill. "And he didn't even find time to check up on our current church-parade status. He's *my* kind of God-botherer!"

The men laughed. Not long after they extinguished their lantern and tried to sleep. In five other tents, the other crews listed for the Salamaua job also did their best not to dwell too much on the day ahead.

It was still dark at 0500 hours as 'B' Flight pilots and navigators crawled from blankets and mosquito nets and donned their shirts, shorts and the favoured army-issue boots. Even at that hour it was too warm for any other layer of clothing. The men assembled near the kitchen where the ever-faithful Lola and Brenda provided toast, powdered eggs and tea, accompanied by warm wishes for their gallant airmen. Then it was down to stores to grab 'chutes, Mae Wests and emergency rations. From there to the utility truck which would take them and their gear to dispersal. As they bounced along the track, Ralph and Bill and their navigators assessed the operation to come.

"I s'pose if we're forming up on 'Blazer' the trip in and out'll be pretty straightforward," Ralph observed.

"Yep – but I've plotted a course anyway," replied Don. "And Met was confident we'd have a clear run – only the usual build-up later on the range to worry about."

"Mmm – that's a plus," agreed Bill. "It mightn't be much chop if we had any weather to contend with on the first job, eh?"

'Blazer' chuckled. "You'll get used to it, old son. Once the first op's under your belt it's like ducks to water. That's not to say Salamaua is a piece of piss. Stan was right on the money at briefing – the Nips'll be shooting back, sure as eggs. They don't seem to like our efforts to put holes in their stuff." He grinned. "But if we do it right we'll be home and hosed. Ack-ack'll only have a few minutes to open up and it won't be concentrated." 'Blazer's' confidence was reassuring to the new airmen, especially combined with the fact that he'd been on and come back in one piece from quite a few previous shows.

The ute rolled into the dispersal area where camouflage netting stretched on poles and tree branches above the Beaufighters. Each huge beast, patient and brooding in its earth-brown and foliage-green skin, looked as truculent as ever. Their general purposeful air helped to reinforce 'Blazer's' recent words. The twelve men shouldered equipment and leaped from the ute. In pairs they headed for their machines as groundcrew scampered about in the early morning greyness, conferring final pre-flight touches. Some fliers took the customary option of watering the tail-wheel, not only to relieve pre-action bladder build-up, but also for luck. It was an old tradition. A few men dashed into the tall kunai to empty bowels. No one flew with demands of nature unanswered if he could possibly help it!

Then it was up the nose ladders for pilots and through the belly-access for the navs. With 'chutes stowed and harness fastened, each pilot began pre-flight checks for his machine. A fitter slowly cranked the huge three-bladed Rotol props to spread oil through crankcases and cylinders. In their cockpits pilots went through the unforgettably ribald pre-flight mnemonic, along the lines of 'Tickling Mary's Fanny With A Sixpence …' Elevator and rudder trim was set; mixture in full-rich position; propeller pitch in full fine. Correct fuel tanks were selected; gills opened for running engines on the ground. Then a fitter plugged in the portable battery to fire each engine in turn. He gave a thumbs-up to his pilot who then called: 'All clear – contact starboard!' and pressed the starter button. The 1,560 horsepower Hercules XI on his right coughed, shuddered, then revved and roared. The same procedure with the port motor proved it equally eager to take the ten tons of aeroplane into its natural element. With tail-wheel unlocked for taxiing, a crewman pulled aside chocks. One by one, Beaus nosed forward, taking their turn on the taxiway for the main strip. The rickety tower signalled with its green light to each pilot. 'Blazer' took off first and quickly following, the other five machines made a good start to the sortie. Ralph and Bill were relieved to see the hill on the port side of the strip slide rapidly beneath as they lifted – any swing near the bloody thing and it was likely to be curtains.

At 1,000 feet, the six Beaufighters moved into a loose vic formation, led by 'Blazer' at the point. Just behind and to his left flew Bill and Phil's plane, with Ralph and Don on the opposite side. The Flight climbed steadily, on track for the north coast, and the Owen Stanley foothills moved slowly astern as cruising speed of 160 knots was maintained. The now-familiar olive scrub, grey-green forest growth and endless undulations below held few fears now for Ralph and Bill and their navigators, nor were they worried by the big cauliflower cumulus they knew they'd find later on the mountain crests. Steadily climbing, every airman was confident his machine would have no trouble clearing the 13,000-foot summits without hanging on props.

"We're on our way, Don!' called Ralph on the intercom. "Sky looks good, eh?"

"Sure does, Ralph. And 'Blazer's' flying a pretty accurate heading. I reckon we're spot-on at the moment."

In their aircraft opposite, Bill and Bernie were also chatting to each other, like every other crew, doing their best to dissipate the tension of impending and unavoidable danger.

No one spoke to another crew – they all knew too well the risk of betraying their presence to a listening enemy. The Yanks, unfortunately, often entertained different ideas; on a combined op the Australians had no choice but to put up with an almost non-stop stream of American chatter as they approached or flew out of a target area.

With the peaks of the Owen Stanleys beneath them, each airman intensified his scan of the surrounding grey skies – to port, starboard, ahead, behind, above and below. At any hint of a bandit in the area, the pilot who'd spotted it would simply click his radio button to alert the others. And the closer they drew towards the northern coast of New Guinea, the harder the men peered, especially into and around the red globule of the easterly sun just above their horizon.

With hundreds of nautical miles behind, the six Beaufighters began descending, following the falling terrain and heading for the Huon Gulf and their way point, Lasanga Island. Their course, as Don had observed, was true – ahead and out from the coast lay the island, the sun low on their starboard beam. Above a little scattered stratus, the sky shone pearly pink-grey in the early day. 'Blazer', as they had expected, took them in a shallow dive to treetop level. Airspeed was increased to 200 knots. The six machines skimmed the channel between the mainland and Lasanga Island, flew to seaward for a few more minutes, then banked to port. They were beyond the sight of observers on the mainland and, all going to plan, would come into the Salamaua Isthmus out of the morning sun.

Scanning instruments, each pilot double-checked that safety was 'off' on his firing-button. Behind him, the navigator made final adjustments on the cumbersome F24 camera used to record the attack and the results. Some pilots and navs closed the armour doors between them, figuring to spare the pilot in the event of air or ground fire hitting the man in the rear seat. Other crews, having discussed the matter, left the doors open – the implicit agreement that if one bought it they both did … Ralph and Don and Bill and Bernie belonged to the second group.

'Blazer' is turning to port now, 500 feet off the deck. The others follow. The sun is directly astern and the enemy coast dead ahead. 'Blazer' opens his throttles and the other pilots do the same. At 230 knots the Beaufighters close on the Salamaua Isthmus. They can see the mountaintops inland, with Wau's 4,000 foot peak dominant. The thin smudge of the Salamaua treeline appears and every man focusses on it and the air around. No sign that the enemy is aware, no dots in the sky. Two nautical miles offshore, 'Blazer' leads the Flight into a short climb. Then they fan out into rough line abreast, with Ralph and Bill on either side of their leader's machine. The first sign of shore equipment becomes visible on the Isthmus – sheds, fuel dumps, a few vehicles. Throttles are pushed through quadrants to their maximum; the Beaus dive for a few seconds then, as one, came in at their target. Suddenly the air begins filling with little eruptions of black, ripping the air ahead of the six aircraft. The Japanese are a wake-up. But now at 200 feet altitude and 400 yards out, the leading aircraft are in range of the shore: 'Blazer' swoops, fires and pulls away to port. Ralph and Bill see, fleetingly, the gouts of earth and smoke raised by his burst;

then they are pressing firing buttons. The barrage of their cannons and machine-guns clangs around them. Even at 230 knots, each Beau seems to lose speed for a few moments with that huge recoil. They stop firing as the Isthmus zooms beneath and bank to port. The air behind is thick with ack-ack bursts. Now for the airfield a few miles inland. Still no hint of bandits ahead. They skim the trees then a white cruciform appears among them, with little lumps of revetments and dispersal bays. 'Blazer' pulls up. The others follow suit, then all dive. Again the air around fills with those silent, angry black bursts. In that tiny moment of time six pilots choose a target and fire. Their projectiles rake the airfield, buildings, dispersed aircraft and blast pens. Don suddenly shrieks on the intercom: "Oh God – God – he's hit! Smokin' – goin' down! He's had it! Jesus bloody Christ!" Five aircraft have cleared the enemy strip and are fleeing inland, for home.

'Blazer' is on the radio straight away. He calls for a response from each pilot. There are four answers. Jack Stanton doesn't come in.

'Blazer' is terse: "Looks like Jack didn't get clear. George thinks he saw him hit the trees. Any other sightings?"

Various brief replies in the negative come from two other pilots. It is Ralph, Don's words still drilling into his mind, who confirms George's report. At that height and over that terrain, there is no chance of survival. Sombrely, the airmen form up on their Flight Leader, flying southwest and climbing to return over the range. There are no further radio exchanges.

At Moresby, 'B' Flight landed without incident, and after dispersing aircraft the weary fliers climbed out. Each crew walked around its plane, looking for any signs of damage inflicted over Salamaua. Both Ralph and Bill spotted .5 inch holes in wing undersurfaces and made mental notes to report them to their riggers. Then they gathered under 'Blazer's' aircraft for a grim recap of the morning.

"Wouldn't ya fuckin' know it!" spat 'Dinger' Bell. "Those poor bastards'd only done two or three strikes …"

"A bad show all right," agreed 'Blazer'. There was little else to add until de-briefing with their IO, Stan McInnes, thirty minutes later. It took place in his large tent, flaps raised to admit some air into the stifling space. The dog-tired men gave Stan as much information as they possessed.

"All right – we've got one Nick and two Bettys destroyed on the field. Two big dumps left burning on the Isthmus. Several buildings and vehicles strafed. No explosions. And no fighters got up. Good-oh – we caught 'em napping for once. Or as much as we've been able to," Stan added quickly, remembering that the Japanese hadn't been taken entirely by surprise. "Poor Jack and Sandy – we'd have to accept they're definitely goners. You say you saw flames, George?" the IO repeated.

"Yeah, afraid so, Stan."

'Splitpin' Warnes made an appropriate entry in the Squadron records, from which 'Ace' would compose his letter to the dead men's families. It was a bad prelude to Christmas, 1942.

But like the war, camp life at June Valley continued. Though two or three strikes took place each week leading up to December 25th, the men of 30 Squadron and their related units went about festive preparations with a will. Various stills hidden around Moresby were in full production mode brewing up 'jungle juice', or as the Yanks termed it, 'moonshine likker'. It was potent and popular. If General Blamey had known the half of what was being concocted and consumed at Port Moresby, he'd have had kittens. So much for his 'alcohol-free island'!

One strike on the Kumusi River Bridge near Lae was flown on Christmas Day, but for the rest of the Squadron it was church parade at 0730 hours. The men turned out in full kit, including gas masks, tin hats and weapons, for 'Ace' to open proceedings with the lesson. Padre Kirk followed, his blessedly brief sermon exhorting the Squadron to pursue their war with zeal, courage and glory – and no doubt provide plentiful material for his little book.

Then the parade dismissed for lunch in the Airmen's Mess. Here the officers and senior NCOs had – with Lola and Brenda's willing connivance – prepared a surprise. This was Christmas Dinner, but what a dinner! Roast pork, roast turkey with apple sauce, diced potatoes and green peas. Sweets were equally wondrous: tinned fruit salad, cream and ice-cream. And enough bottled beer to provide one full mug for each man.

Owen Fenwick, the Squadron musician, played appropriate songs on a piano borrowed for the occasion from the nearby Works Unit. Singing began, soon developing into bawdier ballads, then descending to boisterous caterwauling. The ubiquitous jungle juice, and to a lesser extent, the beer, had made rapid inroads on Squadron personnel. Perhaps the only sober men at the time were teetotallers and the three crews returning from the loss-free bridge strike that morning.

Bill dragged out his battered ukulele and in a fuzzy minute or two did his best to tune it. This proved more complex than anticipated. Soon came derisory shouts of encouragement and impatience from his comrades.

"Use some tiger gut, mate! Ya strings've obviously had the Richard!"

"That's because he's been fishin' with 'em!" yelled someone else.

"Orright, orright – pipe down, you buggers," bawled Bill. "I think she's right – just about …" And he strummed a chord. A semi-silence fell on the men, and Bill used it to launch into his *'Chrissy Ditty for 'Ace'.*

> *It's Chrissy time here in Goon Valley,*
> *With Aussie too far away,*
> *The Japs haven't been very pally –*
> *The buggers're determined to stay.*

But 'Ace' and his boys're responding
With tons of good reason to leave –
They'll go in so low in a beautiful Beau
And cause good ol' Tojo to grieve ...!

The cheering assembly lustily echoed the final two lines, then mugs, glasses and even tea-cups filled to the brim with dire alcoholic substances were raised and quaffed.

Bob Bennett and Ross Small, valiantly attempting to continue their ongoing table-tennis tournament, accidentally flattened the last intact ball and had to temporarily suspend hostilities. This was just as well, as during their final few games each man had been using the table more as a prop for his tottering self than as a sporting arena!

Bill, meanwhile, had discarded his sadly out of tune instrument and was climbing the main pole of the Mess – minus trousers. He'd bet Ralph that he could reach the top and remain there for five minutes. At the two-minute mark Ralph won the bet. He was markedly assisted by Bill's alcoholic ballast and the fact that every man there was pelting the climber with anything in reach. The tall ruckman slowly and swearingly slid groundwards where he was set upon by cheering comrades, hoisted shoulder high and dumped outside, still without pants. The party had warmed up well – and the New Year was still to come!

5

GOLDEN IN THE HEYDAYS

"Crikey! – what's that racket?" said Ralph to Don as they relaxed on the long-drop latrines in the cool evening of December 31st.

"Dunno," said Don. "Sounds like small arms fire. Can't be the Japs – they're nearly back at Gona by now."

The airmen continued listening as distant popping, like an insane jumping jack, grew in frequency. As fast as possible Ralph and Don disengaged themselves from the latrine boxes and prepared to investigate. Just as they made their way past the hessian screen an erratically weaving jeep careered into view. It was loaded with a motley assortment of Australians, some waving bottles and several firing pistols into the dusk. Luckily the barrels were pointed more or less skywards. The jeep, with much over-revving and the odd clash of gears, skidded past. Its inebriated crew screamed, between volleys, "Happeee New Yeeeah!"

Don looked at his watch. "The silly galahs're five hours early!"

"Yeah – and they'll be in a fine old condition to see in '43, eh, Don?" said Ralph, grinning.

Then, as it had done on and off all day, the rain came down in big heavy dollops and the pair dashed for their tent. The jungle-juice needed checking, in any case.

Seeking shelter in the Mess tent Bob and Phil helped themselves to a cuppa and looked back on their first two months in 30 Squadron. Since their sortie to Madang they had flown strikes on average once a fortnight.

"It wasn't too choice doing over that supply column, was it, Bob?" said Phil ruminatively.

"No fear, mate. You don't mind giving the Nips a burst, but when it's poor bloody animals ..." Bob remembered too clearly how they and three other Beau crews had strafed a line of pack mules bringing up Japanese supplies from Kokoda in their push for Moresby. The mules had no chance of escape on the narrow hillside trail, though their human drivers would probably have gained cover.

"We must've destroyed a lot of their equipment," Bob reflected, "but it still leaves a nasty taste in your mouth. Ages ago I read a book set in the First War, in France. *Quiet on the Western Front*, or something, by a bloke on the Jerry side. He describes artillery fire catching horses in the open. One of the Jerries, who'd been a farmer before the war, goes troppo when he sees what's happening to the animals – which get pretty well shot to bits. If I remember, the poor bastard takes it so badly that he skedaddles. They catch him and he's tried as a deserter ..."

"Thank Christ we don't have to get too close to the results of what we do, eh, Bob," commented Phil.

"You've said it, cobber. A 20 mil shell can cause some strife, no doubt about it. I'd hate to be on the receiving end of one!"

Above and around the rain continued to drum on the Mess.

Over in their canvas castle Bill and Bernie were keeping a close eye on a batch of juice. It was brewing nicely.

"She'll be corker!" said Bernie. "Those raisins did the trick, I reckon. It'll be a real do tonight – but I wish this ruddy rain'd give it a rest."

They peered through their tent opening at the silver-white torrent outside. The annoying thing was that, as a rule, Port Moresby didn't get much rain. Now, just when the Squadron wanted a big celebration, nature decided to let go.

But wet or no wet the New Year was going to be ushered in with a wing-ding. In every tent, tin shed, work hut and the Messes, an incredible variety, quality and quantity of alcohol found its way down eager throats. Singing (if it can be so generously described), cards, games and hi-jinks, often as not concluded in the saturating rain, continued up to the midnight hour.

Then the countdown began – on the stroke of twelve the racket went up. All over Moresby ack-ack guns, deeply resonating horns from ships in the harbour, sirens, rifles and handguns erupted with furious abandon, well into the early hours of 1943. Some of the engineers even set off a charge of gelignite they'd prepared especially. The New Year entered with a bang!

But there was also a war to be organised, and sorties continued. Early in January four Beaus left for a barge-sweep near Salamaua. Bruce Stephens radioed not long after take-off to report a fault in his rudder system. He decided to turn back to Ward's. Having insufficient rudder input to control yaw, Stephens swung on the last stage of his flare above the strip, drifted to starboard and hit the trees. With a frightful, tearing crunch, the plane collapsed, erupted in flame and burned and burned. The pilot and his navigator had no chance. Their helpless comrades at the strip could only gape in horror as the blazing Beaufighter incinerated its crew.

The enemy inflicted his share of destruction as well. Two weeks into January Lightnings succeeded in chasing away a Flight of Japanese bombers but a few nights afterwards the Bettys came back to Moresby. This time the P-38s hadn't got up early enough. Bombs exploded only 200 yards from the Operations Room at the eastern end of June Valley. Then two nights later raiders dropped daisy-cutters on Jackson's Strip and blew apart a 'biscuit bomber' loaded with supplies intended for forward Australian troops.

Later in January, once more at night, the Japanese returned. Only three this time but despite every attempt by the Lightnings to engage, bombs hit smack on the 'B' Flight dispersal area. As dawn lit their campsite, men headed down to the strip to inspect the damage.

"Christ Almighty!" said Vic Watchman to 'Dinger' Bell, "they've done over our kite!"

"The little buggers!" added Bill. "And looks like a few more in dispersal've copped it. Tojo's not givin' up in a hurry, eh?"

A balm for battered spirits was the timely arrival of *All In Fun* at the end of January. This show by the Middle East Concert Party arrived in Moresby fresh from Egypt, Palestine, Syria and Transjordan. For one afternoon and evening, the Murray Barracks Hall reverberated with swing music, dance and sketches – enough to hearten many hitherto weary airmen.

Back in their tent in June Valley after the jollity, Bob and Phil hauled out the venerable wind-up gramophone and played their entire collection – two 78s which had seen better days. The hymns *Abide With Me* and *Lead, Kindly Light* filtered through the late still evening, seeming to calm even the mosquitoes. Many 30 Squadron men slept more peacefully that night than they'd done for weeks.

Then in the war's wider scheme the strategic situation began to heat rapidly. January's raids by the Japanese hadn't been random, not by any means. All recce and coastwatcher gen pointed to the enemy mustering strength at Rabaul. There, Simpson Harbour filled with shipping – tramp steamers, transports, barges and several types of naval craft, large and small. Having retreated on the Kokoda Track to defeat at Buna-Gona and Sanananda in December, Hirohito's forces were resolved to regain the initiative. But US Intelligence, using its 'Magic' intercepts, had broken the

Japanese Naval code and gained advance notice of most opposition moves in the Pacific. They now knew that their enemy planned to reinforce his garrisons at Lae, Salamaua and Madang, then make another push for Moresby. What to do about the threat, that was the rub …

Throughout February of '43, the intelligence flowed into HQ. MacArthur's USAAF Commander, General George C. Kenney, knew he had to counter Japanese ambitions. The navy was stretched to its limit in the Solomons – all he had to throw into the ring were the Allied aeroplanes. Kenney conferred through long meetings with RAAF Group Captain Bill Garing to make plans.

"For Chrissake, Bill – we don't wanna piss away men and airplanes in scattered attacks like we've been doin' so far!" The General was concerned.

"Couldn't agree more, George," said Bill Garing, long christened 'Bull' by his men. "We've got to co-ordinate a sufficient number of aircraft. That means adequate fuelling, arming and communication between groups. When we make our strike, it'll have to be in strength – and decisive!"

"Well, Bill, the mods've been done on the B-25s. 'Pappy's' got 3rd Attack Group fitted with four .50 calibres in the nose and four more on either side of the pilot. We've added full boost on the servo trim tabs – that's in spite of all the flak from our back-room boys. I reckon the Mitchells'll be humdingers in a low-level role!"

"How's progress on the skip-bombing?"

"Keen, Bill, keen! Ed Larner's workin' out tactics for below-masthead approaches. You know we had a problem or two – one collision with the wreck and one damaged airplane when it dropped an instant-fused bomb. But we've got a five second delay on 'em now. An' your Aussie detonators are just the bee's knees!"

'Bull' Garing was already aware of the USAAF's mixed success with its mock runs on the *Pruth*. But he had faith in Kenney, in

'Pappy' Gunn's modified B-25s and in leaders like Major Ed Larner, commander of the American 90th Attack Squadron.

Kenney continued, more soberly. "You realise that the Japs won't exactly be takin' our attack lyin' down? Even if our P-38s engage all the Zekes, the escorts'll be blazin' away with everythin' they've got …"

"Not to mention the ack-ack from the transports. Too right I know! It won't be any picnic for our Beaus – they'll be first in at mast height and copping a hell of a lot of return fire … Yes …But if we can just make the Nips keep their heads down it'll be that much easier for your skip-bombing, eh?" Garing was as optimistic as always.

So the two leaders pored over their maps and data, making estimates, conjectures and projections long into the night. Planning. It was late February, 1943 and a battle loomed which would have enormous repercussions on the course of the Pacific war.

Back at Ward's, every serviceable Beaufighter was in hard training for the anticipated action. Thirty Squadron made run after run on the *Pruth,* the Beau crews polishing low-level gunnery where their B-25 counterparts had rehearsed skip-bombing tactics.

"Strewth – will we ever get it right?" asked Bill when he landed after one of the wreck strafes. "We're just getting in each others' way, Bernie – no bloody room to move!" Pilot and navigator made their way into the Mess and sat.

"You're not wrong," replied Bernie stoically. "But when the Jap convoy arrives we'll have more than one ship to occupy us – enough for everyone, you wait!"

"And a few escort boats as well – not to mention their flamin' top cover …" Bill mused for a moment. "Still, the Lightning boys might even up the equation, eh? Jeez, it's going to be some do!"

Ralph, Don, Bob and Phil came in then, spotted their comrades and approached.

"Gidday, fellas," offered Bill. "Pull up a pew. Lookin' forward to Tojo's arrival?"

"I don't know about that, Tassie," said Ralph, grinning. "Could get a bit hot near those ships. What d'you think, Bob?"

"Well, the Jap'll be pretty confident he'll get through. We've not had a very impressive sink rate on 'em so far, have we?"

"That's because our strikes've been too haphazard," commented Don. "Not enough aircraft to push home an attack."

Phil said: "So far though, we've only tried conventional bombing – high and medium altitude. But this Yank low-level stuff – bouncing their bombs off the water – that might be just the ticket."

"They're sure knocking the living daylights out of the wreck, eh!" added Bernie with warmth. "Looks like the idea could come up trumps."

"That's the devil of it," said Ralph. "Our attacks'll have to be right down the Jap gun barrels. You can bet they'll be chucking the works at us!"

"It's what we're there for," put in Bob. "Our strafing fire should clear the way for the B-25s. If we can just get close enough, in enough force to knock out the ack-ack crews …" He trailed off. Like everyone else, Bob knew those same ack-ack gunners would be doing their utmost to knock *him* out of the sky.

As the rainy steamy February days marched on, conversations, arguments and predictions continued all over June Valley and in the American camps. Then things cranked up several notches. 'Ace' Walters called a briefing for every 30 Squadron pilot and navigator – both his operational Flights. It was the last week of the month.

Ralph, Bill, Bob and their respective oppos joined other keyed-up aircrews chatting with mock insouciance as they found places on the long benches of the Ops Room tent. Every man saw on the rear wall the big chart and blackboard on which had been lettered, large: 'March 1 – 3'. 'Ace' moved in front of the Squadron and tapped his cane a few times on the table beside him. A hush fell in seconds.

"All right, gentlemen, I believe you've all been expecting something. And now, by Jove, you're going to get what you wanted! You know about Tojo's build-up in Rabaul. It's divisional strength and Intelligence informs us it'll be travelling on approximately eight transports, with an equal number of destroyer escorts." There was in instant low hum of comment from the airmen for a moment or two. 'Ace' paused for it then kept on. "We expect Jap top cover as well, flying from Lae and Rabaul. At this stage Intelligence isn't sure if the convoy'll sail along the north or south coast of New Britain. That'll be sorted out soon enough, when they leave. But here's what we are clear about." 'Ace' pointed his cane at the blackboard lettering. "The first few days of March, gentlemen – then it'll be on, mark my words. Ross and 'Blazer' inform me that rehearsals on the wreck're getting better. Seems that what the Yanks've left we've put our share of holes in!" He grinned, and every man in the room grinned with his CO. "May I now say this – with as much emphasis as I am capable? Your job when going for the ships, will be to eliminate return fire *and* to clear the bridges. If we can knock off their commanders, the Nips'll be like headless chooks. Their captains and senior officers run things from the bridge – get them and we're more than halfway there. Do I make myself clear, gentlemen?" There was much nodding, and many emphatic 'yes's' echoed around the Ops Room. No pussyfooting around it; the Beaufighter crews intended to harass, wound and kill their enemy with everything they possessed. No one had any doubts or qualms on that score. They knew that the Japanese felt exactly the same way about them.

'Ace' was continuing. "If this division – between 6,000 and 7,000 men – reaches New Guinea the consequences could be catastrophic. We know that a convoy got through in January with the loss of only one ship. If they pull it off again … Well – then it's Wau, and after that, Moresby. The stakes, gentlemen, are high. But there's a big difference this time. A: the number of aircraft at our disposal is by far the largest we've been able to concentrate to date – nearly a hundred kites if you include top cover. B: the low-level attack strategy looks promising. 'Bull' Garing says the Yanks are tickled pink with their skip-bombing and the .50 calibre guns they've added to some of their planes make 'em nearly as good as ours for strafing. So when those Jap ships come into range, on the western end of New Britain – we pounce. All we'll need is enough good weather …"

'Ace' paused. Everyone remembered how low cloud and squalls, as well as the Allies' piecemeal attacks, had helped the January convoy slip through to Lae. If the clag hung about again the situation might easily be repeated. And the recent nor'easter season rain was giving little respite. They could only hope.

"Yeah – the ruddy weather," 'Ace' continued, divining his men's concerns. "Met's optimistic about it – but I'll let Mike give you the good oil on that in a few ticks. All I ask, gentlemen, is for every one of you to be ready when the time comes. Your aircraft will be fuelled and armed and in dispersal on continual stand-by from now on until our attack. 'A' and 'B' flights are to remain on full alert. Yes, you're keyed-up – I'm in the same boat myself – but try to get plenty of sleep. And for God's sake, keep off the turps!" 'Ace' chuckled. "We'll celebrate *after* we knock off the convoy, eh?" A raucous response of 'Too right!' and 'Bloody oath!' came from the airmen. The Squadron Leader then passed proceedings over to Mike Barnes, his Met Officer, for a weather briefing. The pervasive frontal system was moving through, summed up Mike. They could expect calm, clear conditions for early March. "It may be going the Japs' way at the moment," commented the Met man as everyone glanced at the saturated canvas above, "but give it a day or two – by the beginning of March …"

Sure enough, on the first day of the new month, cloud was thinning and squalls easing. And the latest news from coastwatchers and Cat-boats was that the convoy had left Rabaul, moving along the north coast of New Britain. At least eight transports with seven destroyers and what appeared to be one light cruiser escorting. A sizeable swarm of their Navy or Army Airforce machines flew above them. The temptation to take a swig or three of jungle-juice was great and omnipresent; however most pilots and navigators of 30 Squadron, along with their USAAF counterparts, resisted the craving. The next few days sat far too heavily on their minds.

The padre was in his element, chatting with Squadron personnel, offering various saws encouraging stoic acceptance of danger and making endless entries in his notebook.

Lola and Brenda agog with anticipation, conjectured with delicious apprehension on the approaching battle. "Dear me – pray that they all come back safe and sound!" said Lola to his kitchen companion not long after the briefing.

"Golly, yes! It's not going to be any pushover, is it? Those Japanese will be shooting back …"

"Well," continued Lola with admirable fortitude, "whatever will be, will be." (He'd been talking with the padre.)

On March 2nd, it looked set. The enemy convoy had passed the halfway point on the New Britain coast near Talasea. Catalinas shadowing the ships dropped flares and (without success) the odd bomb at night. Bursts of foul weather persisted through the day and into the evening. Despite this Beauforts from 100 Squadron mounted torpedo attacks on several of the convoy vessels but through faulty equipment, Japanese evasive tactics and poor visibility, they had no luck. By 0800 hours on March 3rd, the convoy reached the westerly tip of New Britain at Cape Gloucester. It rounded the Cape and began steaming out of the Bismarck Sea into the Vitiaz Strait, heading directly for Lae.

0830 hours. "Contact!" From the dispersal bays at Ward's Strip, pilots' shouts went up and again the mighty Hercules engines drummed away dawn stillness. Soon twelve green-brown creatures, fuelled and armed, rolled into position along taxiways. 'A' Flight, led by Ross Small, took off first, with Bob and Phil's Beau among its six machines. The aircraft of 'B' Flight followed, including Bill and Bernie and Ralph and Don, led by 'Blazer'. Standing precariously in the well behind 'Blazer' was the Commonwealth Film Unit cameraman, Damien Parer. He'd been posted to the Squadron after getting some amazing combat footage of the AIF in Africa and on the Kokoda Track. Parer wasn't going to miss out on the convoy attack – no fear!

"The day's looking good," said Don to his pilot as their Beau joined formation above Moresby.

"You're not wrong, mate – sea's like a billiard table," remarked Ralph. "ETA still the same?"

"Yep – 0930 at Cape Ward Hunt," replied Don. "Gawd – just look at that! A few Yanks, eh?"

Ralph couldn't help but notice the cause of Don's awed observation. There were now dozens of aircraft in the air leaving the six strips around Moresby for their north coast rendezvous. Above, a blue-grey sky rapidly filled with machines, the twin-tailed Lightnings blackening the higher altitudes.

Bob and Phil were also in good spirits. "I've never seen so many kites at one time," said Bob to his navigator.

"It's going to be a stoush and a half," replied Phil gleefully. "Just get us home in one piece so I'll have something to write to Lois tonight, eh!"

"I'll do my best, cobber – I'll do my best. Make sure you give us a good course in and back, all right?"

And the airmen, gazing at the silver, foliage-green and earth-brown machines around, kept station with their Australian and American comrades.

Less than an hour later, the northern coast of Papua New Guinea appears; their rendezvous, Cape Ward Hunt, points a stark grey finger into the Huon Gulf. At various levels, with guardian P-38s at the summit, aircraft circle, waiting. There are streams of four-engined Flying Fortresses, their tubbier silver-sided cousins the Liberators, twin-engined Boston attack bombers and the deadly B-25 low-level skip-bombers, some armed with 'Pappy' Gunn's extra .50 calibres. The two Flights of Beaufighters find a slot in the airspace among them. In every occupant of every aeroplane tension and apprehension bind tighter. Many men reckon only half of them will get back.

At last the message they've waited for, terse on the radios: "The game is on. Move out, bearing 040. Repeat – bearing 040." One by one, the circling streams of fighters and bombers straighten, tracking slightly east of north. Above a pellucid, cobalt and grey ocean, they fly among remnants of frontal clouds from the preceding days.

And then on the northern horizon, they sight them – black dots on the water with wobbly pencil smudges stretched out behind. The convoy. As their plan of attack has decreed, the Beaufighters draw ahead to the vanguard of the Allied planes – they are to go in first. In twelve machines, pilots' knuckles tighten on the control spectacles. Gunsights are switched on and set for 200 yards. The dots ahead grow bigger and darker. Aircrews can see the glistening white wakes of the ships now and the slim shapes of eight destroyers leading on either beam of the transports. With throttles eased further forward the aircraft dubbed 'Whispering Death' by their makers begin a shallow dive. They move into a line abreast formation. Now superstructures, masts and funnels are visible on the ships. At a distance of six nautical miles comes the first salvo from the destroyers. It is accurate. The Japanese gunners wait until the Beaus can be engaged in a crossfire; shell-bursts all range within 100 yards of the approaching aircraft. Parch-mouthed, the crews watch great sheets of flame leap from the length of each destroyer as gun after gun fires. On the radios, an uninterrupted stream of excited, inane American chatter: 'Looka that!' 'Go boy!' Yippee!' 'Atta boy!' 'Go get 'em!'

"Those bloody Yanks!" mutters Bill to Bernie on his intercom. "They couldn't shut up for their own mother's funeral!" But like every other Australian pilot closing on the ships, he ignores this running commentary as best he can.

Now the destroyers come around bow-on to the Beaufighters. "They must think we're Beauforts making a torpedo run!" calls Ralph to Don.

"You beaut – they'll have no flanking cover!" replies the navigator. The transports are wide open to a beam attack.

Eight thousand feet above, fighters of each side prepare to engage as the bombers drone into position over the convoy. The Lightnings climb at maximum boost and release their belly tanks for better manoeuverability.

"Good Lord!" yells Ralph. "What on earth –?" as large metal lumps flutter down past their plane.

"It's the Yanks' drop-tanks – hope we don't collect one!" calls Don in reply. This plus the curtain of ack-ack, keeps every Beau pilot more than focussed for the next few seconds. Luckily, neither Americans nor Japanese score any hits.

Now, 2,000 yards away the ships loom large. Skimming the surface the Beaufighters are cyclone fast. The pilots jink to port and starboard, selecting a target. There are plenty – fat and heavy and seemingly frozen on that flat flat sea.

Bob chooses a 7,000 ton transport with goal-post masts and a single funnel. A thick black stream belches out of it. He can see the sparks of a 20mm gun firing at him from the bridge. He stops jinking. At 220 knots Bob holds the bridge centred in his sight. He presses the button. The familiar yammering detonation of cannons and machine-guns echoes for three seconds. The ship flashes beneath and Bob heaves back and banks. Phil yells that they've scored hits – flame and smoke flare from the boat's mid-section. The stream of cannon shells gouges towering plumes of spray from the sea near the ship. Bob climbs and begins turning as Phil, grunting in the ecstasy of his urgency, changes the unwieldy cannon feed drums on each gun. They go in again.

Further into the convoy Ralph and Bill have similarly picked targets. They approach low and hard and throw sheer devastation at the ships. Just as 'Ace' ordered, the bridge is their aiming point. It must be carnage there. The Beau's four cannon and six machine-guns are concentrated in a small box – the result is unequivocal. Nothing can withstand it …

And now the B-25s with their 500-pounders as well as their .50 calibres are coming in, right on the tails of the Beaus. All over the convoy, drawing only token return fire, the bombers fly at the dark wide flanks of transports and escorts. They make hit after hit – tactics the Allies worried about, practised, modified and re-practised are malevolently vindicated.

In the space of fifteen minutes a once-neat pattern of vessels on a tranquil sea wallows in utter chaos. Fires blaze on at least four of the Japanese boats, including a destroyer. Most ships are dead in the water, which is covered with oil, flotsam and survivors. Again and again the Beaus and bombers go in: strafe – bomb; strafe – bomb; strafe – bomb … Higher up the Fortresses and Liberators let go their 1,000-pounders, scoring several hits and near misses and fending off determined fighter attacks as Zekes and Oscars make pass after pass. The heavy bomber waist and turret gunners work their .50 calibres overtime, firing, rebelting and firing again till the barrels glow red. Japanese fighters wound several of the bombers and one B-17 topples into a spin with smoke pouring from her. The crew jumps. One by one the white blossoms of 'chutes open against feathery grey alto-stratus overhead. But those airmen do not reach the sea alive. Several Zeros wheel in on the descending, helpless men and fire. The Americans have no chance.

After his third run on a ship Bill finds all ammo gone and is pulling up when Bernie yells over the intercom: "Bandit closin' – above port quarter!' Immediately the pilot pushes taps to the maximum, diving for the sea.

"He's stayin' with us!" warns Bernie.

Bill races through options. To starboard ahead, a B-25 is turning. He says quickly: "I'm goin' past the Yank in front! If their rear-gunner's a wake-up he'll have a go at the Jap. Might shake 'im off." And Bill flashes past the Mitchell. His guess proves correct. From tail and dorsal turrets of the bomber .50 calibres open up on the Zero. It breaks away to seek less venomous prey. Bill and Bernie release a collective sigh and head southwest for the New Guinea coast and home. Behind them, as ammunition runs out, other Beaufighters and American aircraft do the same. They leave the wreckage of twelve ships, some already sunk completely, others listing and breaking up. Spread across the water is debris, fuel oil and small groups of Japanese soldiers and sailors, dead and alive. One of the most decisive, one-sided encounters in the history of modern warfare is over hardly an hour after it has begun.

They kept radio silence on their return to Moresby, so it wasn't until landing at Ward's and excitedly assembling in the Ops Room that crews could compare experiences.

"It was a rout – an absolute, total rout!" chortled Bill. "Bernie and I lost count of the number of ships on fire."

"Even the destroyers were coppin' it," added Bob. "I saw one go up in a huge burst. His magazine must've caught – hardly anyone could've lived through it."

Ralph said: "Not many of 'em will make it to Lae. This time, they damn well *didn't* have it their own way. Tojo won't be in a hurry to repeat this, you can bet your bottom dollar!"

Just how significant the engagement had been became clearer at de-briefing. The crews who'd taken part met with 'Ace' Walters and their IO, Stan McInnes, soon after the first animated assembly.

'Ace' was beaming, his teeth a white keyboard beneath his trim black moustache.

"A corker show, gentlemen! The gen coming in couldn't be better. Latest estimate is that at least ten of the ships are goners. Not one – I repeat – not *one* transport reached Lae. And all of our crews are back barring Ray and Doug – but they're OK – a few scratches. They had a Nip on their tail in the battle area and copped a bit. They got to the mainland though – brought their damaged kite in at Popondetta. As for Tojo – well, it'd be the understatement of the year to say he's received a very bloody nose indeed. A large part of the credit goes to this Squadron. I might add here that I sneaked across in a spare kite with some of the Lightning boys to keep an eye on proceedings. It was an absolute bottler, a credit to every man-jack of you. Thanks."

Around the Ops Room men looked cheerfully at each other. They were sweat-soaked, filthy and exhausted, but they'd helped in a big way in a big show. As Phil, Bob Scott's navigator, had hoped every airman would indeed have 'something to write home about' to his relatives and friends. The Battle of the Bismarck Sea.

6

OUT OF GRACE

The next day recce of the battle vicinity reported barges, lifeboats and rafts in the water among the convoy debris. They were 25 miles off Cape Ward Hunt. 'Ace' called a briefing.

"I'm sorry, gentlemen – there's a bit more work to do," said the CO. "Not a very pleasant job. It seems quite a few survivors got off the ships. They're in small boats, barges and rafts and as far as we can determine, they're heading for Lae or Salamaua. Thirty Squadron has been ordered to make sure they don't get there – "

"Sir – you mean …?" Ralph couldn't complete his question.

"Yes, Raymond," replied the CO, "we have to shoot 'em. Sink every boat, barge and raft – don't let one man get ashore in Jap territory. The Yanks've asked us to be in on it because our kites are the best for the job. They're sending out their fighters and some of the B-25 strafers as well." 'Ace' hesitated for a few moments. "I can guess what you're thinking gentlemen, but unfortunately there doesn't seem to be any alternative. Most of the Yank navy is tied up at Guadalcanal – we can't get any ships to the area for at least a week. By that time the Japs will've skedaddled."

"It'll be fish in a barrel!" said 'Dinger' Bell with relish.

"Who'd be a Jap on that water?" muttered Bob to Phil. "The poor bastards won't have the ghost of a chance …"

'Ace' went on. "I ask you to keep in mind men, that this is war.

We've been given our orders. We have to follow them to the letter *no matter what personal views we may hold!* There'll be three aircraft from each Flight on patrol tomorrow morning and a new shift in the afternoon. Names are on the Ops Board as of now. That is all – carry on." 'Ace' turned smartly, donning his peaked cap as he bent under the flap of the tent.

"Phew! This is a different kettle of fish," said Ralph to Bob and Bill in the outbreak of comment which followed the CO's exit.

"God, yes," said Bob. "I never imagined we'd be in this position. I joined the RAAF in the first place because – well – because I thought there was a skerrick of decency in a flying war … To strafe blokes who're helpless – hell!"

"But what can we do instead?" asked Bill. "If the Japs reinforce Lae and Salamaua, our AIF boys will have to take 'em on. We get 'em now there's a few less to be shooting at our fellows. That's the way I see it, at least."

"It's a bad business," Ralph said, "whichever way you look at it."

The next morning, as ordered, three Beaufighters fly to the battle area. Bill and Bernie and Ralph and Don are led by 'Blazer'. The weather is again clear, the sea flat calm.

"There's our target," radios the Flight Lieutenant, as from 3,000 feet the crews approach some dark lumps among the slick and flotsam on the water. The pilots alter their echelon formation to line astern and circle. Below, five Type 'B' barges and a lifeboat have formed a small flotilla. Each is packed with men and supplies. The Beau pilots can distinctly see green uniforms on many Japanese in the boats. There is no fire coming at them from the men in the water.

"All right – I'll go in first, then Ralph, then Bill," orders 'Blazer'. "Get close. Don't waste a bullet." The Flight Leader, banking towards the Japanese, comes out of his turn in a shallow dive a few hundred feet above the sea. At 300 yards range he fires. The familiar geysers of spray from his cannon shells dance towards and into the target. Bits of metal and timber and flesh fly out from the centre of 'Blazer's' barrage. The Beaufighter pulls up to join the other two circling machines.

"Your turn, Raymond," comes the call. "There's a few left."

"OK, Don," says Ralph on the intercom, his mouth dryer than it has ever been. "We're going in." Ralph banks towards what is left in the water, descending gradually. He lines up on the target ahead. Two barges are still more or less floating among the wreckage. Ralph and Don can see the churned up sea and foam turning red. Carefully, Ralph aims and presses the button. Again geysers race across the surface towards the Japanese. Ralph and Don zoom above them, climbing and turning.

"Get a bag!" calls 'Blazer' sarcastically on the radio. "You undershot like buggery."

"Sorry, skipper," replies Ralph. "Shall I go 'round again?"

"Nah. Bill'll have 'em. OK, Tassie – see if you can do the job."

"Too right!" comes Bill's reply. And he goes in. The remaining barges disintegrate under the hurricane of his bullets.

"Christ!" observes Bernie on the intercom as they pull up to check the results of their attack. "The sharks'll get a good feed, won't they?"

"Too right, cobber – better them than us, eh!" answers Bill.

After one more circle of the target, the three Beaufighters re-form an echelon and fly home.

That afternoon the same grim job is repeated. Bob and Phil are among the three hunting machines this time, led by Ross Small. They soon find another little flotilla, lifeboats and rafts. The two small boats are under sail attempting to tow the rafts. Every inch of each vessel is crammed with men. For a few pointless seconds, there is a burst of small arms fire from one boat as Ross goes in to strafe. Under the deadly flail of his guns it is quickly silenced.

Once more every boat is shattered, every Japanese killed. Again the pathetic remnants of corpses stain the wreckage and foaming sea crimson.

Bob and Phil don't talk much on the way home. Each man is locked in the close cell of his imagination. What if the boot had been on the other foot? How can we expect a fair go from these blokes from now on? Is this what war really is, when all's said and done?

During the following days facts and figures on the battle continued to flow in from Intelligence. Eight transports and four destroyers definitely accounted for – though earlier estimates had been much higher. Japanese survivors were being rounded up or shot on Goodenough Island, the Trobriands and various other islands in the Solomon Sea. Huge ructions in Rabaul as the tattered remnants of the Japanese 51st Division trickled in. A few hundred men had got ashore at Lae, plucked from the sea by one of their destroyer escorts and by submarine. But of the six to seven thousand-man division which had so confidently sailed from Rabaul at the end of February this was a feeble trickle. It looked like Japanese hopes to take Moresby were gone for good.

MacArthur was cock-a-hoop about it, saying later that the Battle of the Bismarck Sea had been 'the decisive aerial engagement of the war in the South-West Pacific …'

Then Damien's film came back from processing. It was graphic. One night they set up a 16mm projector in the Mess, which quickly filled with Americans and Australians who'd flown in the battle, as well as many who hadn't. Parer had rested his clockwork camera on 'Blazer's' shoulder as they attacked the ships. Viewers could clearly see the gunfire connecting – little flashes on bridges, decks and hulls, as well as the great gouts of spray from cannon shells hitting the sea. Other segments showed flame and smoke billowing out of ships' midsections.

The cameraman had also been along on a 'clean-up' sweep.

His stark black and white footage recorded ruthlessly just what a Beaufighter could do to human beings packed into small vessels.

"Gor blimey – not very pretty, eh?" commented a viewer who hadn't witnessed it at first hand. Some men slipped away at this stage, seeking a place for reflection in the disguise and comfort of the darkness outside. For many – groundstaff, cooks and clerks – the closest they'd been to the sharp end of a war was during the odd bombing raid by the Japanese. The film was stomach-turning.

The next morning Ralph, Bill and Bob were together in the Mess, soon after breakfast. There were no ops that day.

"Poor old Don," Ralph said, "he lost his kai in the middle of our strafe on the lifeboats. And I wasn't much better off … It was a rotten job."

"Hell's bells, Ralph," said Bill, "we had no choice. You've got to accept that shooting those Japs then has stopped 'em shooting our boys later in New Guinea."

Ralph was getting steamed up. "Oh yeah – you could argue that. You could argue any bloody thing you liked! Doesn't make it any easier to do, though – or any more decent or right – "

"Yeah," Bob added, "what if three or four hundred enemy soldiers *did* get ashore at Lae? They'd have bugger all weapons, no ammo or supplies. On the whole they'd be more of a hindrance than a help to the Jap garrison. Whatever way you look at it, we slaughtered those blokes for no good reason. Or no reason that I can see, at any rate!"

"Murder. Cold blooded, ruddy murder!" put in Ralph.

"That's war, Ralph!" said Bill. "Christ – isn't that what the whole damned thing's all about? If you're not in it for keeps, stay out altogether."

Bob cut in. "All right, mate. And what're you going to tell your kids when they ask you back in Aussie – 'Daddy, what did you do in the war?' D'you say: 'Oh, I machine-gunned defenceless men from my aeroplane!'? Please, Bill, don't give me – or let any damned politician or brass hat or God-botherer – give me any more guff about 'just wars' and the 'ultimate goodness of our cause …'"

"There's not much goodness left anymore, is there?" said Ralph, looking through the door of the Mess to the bare soil outside.

It was Bill's turn to be impassioned. "Are you blokes saying we're as bad as the Japs or the Nazis, for Heaven's sake?"

"When it comes down to the ordinary man or woman in those countries," Ralph answered, "I say we *are* the same, under the skin. For good or for bad. Given the right conditions – leaders who drag us into a war – the propaganda and lies that help 'em do it. Then, once you're in, the training and hardening that begins even before you see combat … We *would* become the same as any enemy soldier. For God's sake, haven't we all just proved that?"

"We'd run concentration camps? Use torture? Bayonet people in cold blood? Have you read anything about the Japs in China, Ralph?" asked Bill with exasperation.

"Too right I have!" said Bob before Ralph could reply. "And like Ralph, I say that we were on a par with 'em yesterday. Hell, some of the Yanks I saw in 9 Ops Group last night wanted to go back for *another* crack at those blokes in the water. They reckoned they'd give two months' pay at the drop of a hat to be in a strafing kite doing 'em over!"

"Western Civilization – that's us," said Ralph. "Maybe they got the second part a bit skew-wiff, eh?"

But Bill was unmoved. "Well, you blokes say what you like. In my book, the Japs've had this coming. They've never shown a skerrick of mercy to anyone they've been up against – from Manchuria to Malaya to New Guinea. Why should we feel crook about giving some of it back?"

"That's the whole point I'm trying to make!" said Ralph. "If we let ourselves become butchers as well, then God help the world … How can we preach about the superior values of democracy, Christianity and the rest of it while we keep on with actions like last week? We'd be total shonks – hypocrites – if we tried that one on!"

Bob said slowly, "And when this war's finally over – and God knows we want it to be! – how on earth do we make sure this sort of behavior – on *every* side – doesn't break out again? If we're prepared to accept that the end justifies the means – that is, do *anything* to win – we're planting the seeds for the next war, sure as eggs!"

"Well, mate, we're in the middle of this one at the moment," countered Bill. "What was it old Macbeth said? 'I am in blood stepp'd in so far …'? We've just got to do what we're told – orders're orders. Unless you want to front a court-martial and get sent back south!"

"You've got me there, Bill," said Ralph. "Not many of us'd be prepared to stick our necks out that much … It's a fair bastard, isn't it?"

"My oath, mate – my bloody oath!" agreed Bob. "Once those dogs of war get on the loose, there's no telling *who* they'll go for."

"And just who – or what – can keep 'em tied up for good, eh?" mused Ralph. "That's the guts of it, isn't it? From the beginning of time, whether they use a stone axe or a ruddy thousand-pounder, human beings seem hell-bent on knocking each other off!"

"You're not wrong, old son!" said Bill, nodding. "Maybe we'll never get it out of our systems – something in the blood, Macbeth or no Macbeth!"

Bob clapped a hand on Bill's broad shoulders. "Jeez, it's a dry argument all right. Let's cool off with a drop of plonk. Phil an' I've got a fresh batch in the tent – reckon we could all do with a snort!"

Appreciatively, the others agreed and followed Bob to his tent in the kunai for a mug of jungle-juice. It provided welcome – if only partial – anaesthetic for an inflamed and aching conscience.

7

TIME HELD ME GREEN AND DYING

Post-battle unease receded further the following day. That morning someone from Mobile Works Section wired up a latrine seat with a megga contact and waited until 'Splitpin' Warnes was comfortably settled. Then, from the end of the wire where he'd hidden himself nearby, the culprit gave his generator handle a hefty crank. 'Splitpin's' outraged yell could be heard all over June Valley …

And there were always the Army nurses to try to get around – and get on with. Some of the less-successful Lotharios chose an embarrassing tactic in retaliation. Knowing the hospital changed shifts at three every afternoon and that the nurses had to travel past the ablution area, these men elected to take a shower just at that time. Somehow, they forgot to wear their towels draped, sarong style, around their waists. 'Look what you sheilas are missing out on!' seemed to be the general message.

Perhaps the same men were jealous of 'Casanova' Collins' success with the nurses. It was no surprise to onlookers when the Army Liaison Officer and his latest conquest boarded Collins' jeep one evening. As the couple departed, the captain's tent – poles, fly and all – came crashing down and pursued the vehicle. The bystanders had connected everything with a hidden rope to its rear axle … There was much mirth from all concerned – with the exception of the jeep's occupants.

Of course, the men grabbed *anything* to relieve the monotony of their food. For despite the best of Lola and Brenda's culinary ministrations, tinned bullamacow, powdered eggs and a variety of dehydrated foodstuffs made a dreary, bland and occasionally nauseating diet. Canned butter was often totally rancid while the dried potatoes, arriving in a glue-like resinous mess, had to be soaked for at least eight hours before cooking.

"You wouldn't read about it," mourned Bob to Ralph and Bill while they waited in the line for midday kai. "The bloody Yanks've set up an *ice-cream* machine at Jackson's! I've heard they even get fresh maple syrup to go with it …"

"That does it," said Bill. "Time for another scrounge, eh, fellers?"

"Too right, sport!" agreed Bob, with Ralph nodding in ready accord.

"The truck and corner tactic?" Ralph asked.

"Yeah – works every time," laughed Bill.

That very afternoon, Bill borrowed a jeep (which itself had been scrounged from the USAAF a month earlier and quickly re-painted with 30 Squadron markings). The three friends took it bumping along the track which led to the American supply depots in Moresby. Selecting a spot where the narrow road wound through the bordering scrub and trees they stopped. While Bill lifted the bonnet of the jeep, Ralph and Bob took up vantage-points in the bushes on the bend. They knew that the Yank supply trucks would have to slow down considerably along this section of their journey to Jackson's and other US campsites. Patiently they waited.

Soon after from up track came revving and rattling. A US olive-drab light truck hove into view through the scrub. Bill, having already sabotaged the jeep's engine, gave his best impression of mechanical bafflement. Ralph and Bob, well hidden, prepared to strike. The truck decelerated, then stopped with a grind of handbrake as Bill waved to its driver. This man, a tall negro in dungarees and forage cap, jumped from the cabin with a cheerful, "Howdy. You havin' trouble there?"

"Too bloody right, mate," replied Bill in mock disgust. "How you blokes get these things to behave is beyond me! Reckon you can have a look at it for us? Could be the carby."

The black man obligingly began examining the innards of the jeep while Bill offered as much misleading and delaying information as he could concoct. Meanwhile, at the rear of the truck, Ralph slipped up under the tarp and began passing out cases and cans to the waiting Bob. The raiders worked quickly and efficiently, favouring the more exotic food labels. They soon had a sizeable hoard cached in the roadside scrub. Ralph slid out of the truck, re-tied the tarp and hid with Bob beside their booty.

The jeep started and Bill drove it to the side of the track after thanking his unsuspecting helper. As soon as the truck had moved on up the road towards one of the US campsites, the bushrangers began loading their vehicle with spoils.

"This'll hit the spot for the next few days, eh?" commented Bob, holding aloft a can of fruit salad as eloquent proof.

"And not a moment too soon!" said Bill. "One more meal of pregnant goldfish and I'd just about turn *into* one of the blasted things …!"

The feast that night went a long way towards ameliorating the strange mix of elation and gloom which permeated June Valley since the Bismarck Sea and its aftermath. Some of the men – aircrew and groundstaff – had been in Moresby since November the previous year without leave. It was now April of '43 – and months in a front line tropical area, with unrelenting rain, humidity, mosquitoes, malaria, tinea, multifarious insects, not to mention the food – had taken an inevitable toll on morale. Perhaps there would be new postings soon, with the six-month tour time nearly expired. The men in Servicing Flight, whose days began at 0600 and ended at 1830 hours, were in desperate need of a rest. Little did they or many others know that 9 Ops Group was at least 1,000 airmen under its authorized strength. Talk about running a war on a shoestring.

Then the Japanese came over. It was morning smoko time in June Valley when a Yellow Alert went up. This warned of enemy raiders twenty minutes out. All over Moresby men donned tin hats and headed for their slit trenches. There was no panic – at least not until the size of the attacking force became clear. Looking skyward they could see at least 40 bombers and even more fighters with one detachment appearing to target Ward's itself. Ack-ack went berserk, its shrapnel falling like hot rain, as the Japanese dropped daisy-cutters along the northern end of the strip. This type of bomb exploded and scattered shrapnel just above ground level. It became a giant, malevolent scythe – if a man was out of his trench when one went off …

The risk factor rose considerably at June Valley when 'Splitpin', complete with tin hat, gasmask, haversack and Smith and Wesson revolver, went into action. In long, jerky strides he dashed about the camp, waving his pistol and shouting: "Don't panic! Don't panic! I'll shoot the first man who panics!" One or two of the airmen anxiously observing the situation from nearby slit trenches seriously contemplated shooting their Adjutant before he shot one of them!

Fortunately neither friendly nor enemy attention caused casualties. It was a different story for the aircraft dispersed at the strip. Bob Bennett's kite was cactus and Chas and Ed found their machine punctured by dozens of holes in the fuselage. George and Eric's plane suffered perforated wings. Obviously, the Japanese were out to avenge the Bismarck Sea. Their Bettys, Sallys and Mitsubishi Zeros still packed plenty of wallop.

So many damaged machines meant that the Squadron would

be out of action until enough planes could be repaired or replaced. More frantic work for the hard-pressed fitters and riggers.

Just before Anzac Day it was on again, with a strike on enemy supply-lines at Komiatum. Four Beaus took off that morning and returned safely just under three hours later.

To mark Easter Sunday the CO ordered a formal parade for the entire Squadron. 'Splitpin' was in his element. He drew up an impressive Order of Service, including the National Anthem, an Invocatory Prayer, General Confession, the Apostles' Creed, a hymn *Abide With Me*, the Lesson (from 'Ace' himself), the Chaplain's address (delivered by Reverend Kirk) and the Blessing. At 0700 sharp on the day of the parade the Adjutant looked at the weather. Scanning a satisfactorily blue sky he suddenly stopped, eyes bulging. "Who in the –? Why, I'll have the blighter skinned alive …!"

Poor 'Splitpin' had spied a substitute for the ensign – hanging from the parade-ground flagstaff was a divinely white, lacy and very femine pair of panties. By 0705 hours, the offending item was replaced. The pantie-planter was never apprehended …

Hi-jinks continued between strikes. Bill managed to get hold of a precious bottle of whisky brought up by a new crew, but not having been able to sample the heady spirit for months, promptly got a little 'squiffy'. One thing led to another and when Bill and 'Dinger', blind drunk, staggered between tents bellowing, "'Ace's' an ass!" it all came to a head. The miscreants were collared and the following morning Adjutant Warnes paraded them outside the CO's tent in full kit – webbing, haversack, sidearms and steel helmets. For an hour Bill and 'Dinger' sweated in the sun, internally and externally, while 'Ace' evinced much interest in the bumph at his table. Then the Squadron Leader called them to attention, turned on a full blast roasting and concluded the episode. There would be no further consequences – or reocurrences!

In early May, eight Beaufighters accompanied B-25s in a strike on Madang and were intercepted by fighters as well as the usual intense ack-ack. Keith and Ken's machine was slightly damaged, copping some Zeke bullets and George and Eric's kite connected with a burst of ground fire. They all got back though, after thoroughly shooting up the target.

A week later news came of a Japanese convoy near Arawe, on the southwest coast of New Britain. Was it going to be another Bismarck Sea? A combined force of Fortresses, Mitchells and Beaufighters was sent to intercept the ships. Bill and Bernie flew with the six Beaus. This time, however, luck was on the Japanese side. Despite a rigorous search along the coast by the Allied aircraft they found no sign of a vessel. Reluctantly their op was declared a fizzer and the planes turned for home.

Halfway back, crossing the Huon Gulf at 13,000 feet, Bill calls: "Bernie, take a dekko to starboard – about two o'clock, on the surface."

"Uhhh … yeah, yeah! Hell, Bill, is it a sub?"

"Let's get down a bit," replies the pilot, at the same time taking 'safety' off his guns. Increasing revs, Bill eases the Beau into a steep dive. At 3,000 feet, pilot and navigator see several men frantically working to bring a deck gun to bear on them.

"Japs for sure!" calls Bill. He continues diving, aiming to level out short of the sub and rake its deck. The first black puffs appear close by, but Bill is descending too quickly for them to be accurate. At over 200 knots, only feet above the ocean, Bill levels out. The sub's conning tower is near centre in his gunsight. He fires and a hail of bullets races along the decking into the gunners and the hull. The sub flashes beneath and Bill banks steeply, hauling the Beau over for a second pass. Bernie yells: "They're diving! Get in again – quick as you can!" Bill drags the heavy machine around with every bit of his strength. Eventually he is on target, coming again at the now half-submerged vessel. One five-second burst along the deck, pull-up, and …

"They're gone, Bill," laments Bernie. "Reckon we've lost the blighters." They circle the bubbling mass of water searching for a sign that their attack has brought results. No debris. Only the thin, dark shadow of the sub heading away southwest.

"Ah well – we frightened the be-Jesus out of 'em, at any rate," observes Bill. "Let's get back."

The next month proved disastrous. 'Darling buds of May' faded quickly with violent death in constant attendance – so often life's precious lease had 'all too short a date …'

On the May 8th six Beaus led by 'Grumpy' Edgerton were scheduled for a strike on Lae. Ralph and Don went on this sortie. Set-up was standard – the Flight crossed the Owen Stanleys and followed the Markham Valley towards the large enemy coastal base and airstrip. Approaching the small hill near Jacobsen's Plantation they fanned out into line abreast formation. Ralph remembered 'Grumpy' to his right as they reared over the final crest, ramming noses down to cover the strip with strafing fire. Ack-ack was instant and fierce and it tracked each aircraft on approach and over the strip. Ralph saw 'Grumpy' getting lower and lower then simply fly into the ground and disintegrate in a massive explosion and fireball. Pilot and navigator would have been killed instantly.

The other five machines and crews got back to Moresby unharmed. For the entire return journey every man silently went over what had happened to 'Grumpy' and Rick. At one time, Ralph had thought it could never happen to him and Don. No. After all, he had always carried out a thorough pre–flight. He flew carefully – never swung on take-off or had any hairy landings. He kept formation accurately, maintained a sharp and conscientious lookout in the air. But none of this mattered. Now, he'd come to the stark realisation – he was as vulnerable as the next man. He too could end up in a flaming metal coffin or beneath the ocean or in Japanese hands… God yes. It was a scenario he tried to keep at bay, to disguise with a myriad of distractions. But not for long. Never for very long.

At the end of the month a batch of fresh crews came up. They all took turns at the customary mock weapons attack on the *Pruth.* One run was led by a pair of new pilots carrying two tyro oppos in the lead Beau. No one knew exactly what went wrong, but for some reason – perhaps a misperception of speed and distance – the first machine aimed at the bow of the wreck, failed to clear its forward mast and clipped it with the starboard wing. A burst of flame from the motor, the wing sheared off and what was left plunged into the sea near the *Pruth.* The two men up front were killed, but by some miracle the navigators survived with only minor cuts and bruising and were picked up by the rescue launch.

In early June, following briefing for an attack on enemy-held villages Kiapit and Boana, eight Beaufighters began a mid-morning take-off. Several aircraft had left Ward's then Sid Woollett started his run. With its throttles wide open and nearly at separation speed, the Beau's port tyre suddenly blew. The aircraft slid sideways, collapsed onto its wing and hurtled along the runway. At the end of the strip it somersaulted and erupted into flames. In seconds the nose section was a pyre of heat and smoke; the helpless rescue crew could get nowhere near Sid. The shattered machine's rear fuselage didn't ignite and helpers carefully pulled out the navigator, Bob Hazelton. He was rushed to the Medical Recovery Station, where he hung on for three agony-filled days. But Bob's terrible internal injuries, taken when his body hit the navigation table, were too much. He died.

Then 30 Squadron farewelled the leader who'd seen it through so much. With his tour as CO expired, Wing Commander Brian 'Ace' Walters was posted south and replaced by Clarrie Trebilcock. It was under Trebilcock that the Beaufighters moved to a new base of operations later in June. The Allies intended to take the air war closer to the Japanese – and a relocation on the very doorstep of the enemy had been selected. The new home was part of the D'Entrecasteaux Island group, at the southeastern tip of New Guinea not far from Milne Bay. Their particular island was called Goodenough, apparently after an early English explorer. Naturally, the Squadron hoped it would live up to its name!

While the site at Goodenough was being readied, 30 Squadron and her sister Boston Squadron, No 22, flew to Milne Bay. They would operate temporarily from there. A thousand and one items – vehicles, fuel, ammunition, provisions, spares and the rest had to be ferried to Goodenough on small cargo boats.

At Milne Bay, which they called Fall River then, it rained almost non-stop. Engineers had laid down steel matting along Turnbull Strip to prevent aircraft bogging in the inevitable mud. On either side of the long metal pathway stood sentinel coconut palms. Through the constant downpour, all a pilot could see were two dark blurs with a slightly clearer space between them.

"Strike me pink!" said Bob to Phil as they joined circuit on their first approach to the new base. "I'm just going to aim our kite at the gap in the trees. Can hardly see a thing in this flamin' murk!"

Thirty squadron set up its tents in a coconut plantation between an American Army unit and No. 6 Hudson Squadron. CO of the Hudsons was Wing Commander Bill 'King' Lear, adorned with a crown of red hair and moustache. The 'King' had dubbed his group the 'Fiery Mo' Squadron and ordered each airman to cultivate a moustache. This proved, in a few cases, less than practical as the younger men were unable to produce more than a dozen downy hairs on their upper lip!

At the first meal they shared with the Hudson boys, Ralph, Bill and Bob were astonished as 'King' Lear entered the room with his men all standing stiffly to attention. Only after the CO had seated himself were his officers permitted to follow suit.

"Good God," whispered Bill to his companions, "who does this joker think he is?"

When they heard that 'King' Lear also kept several chooks, from which he took eggs exclusively for himself, the 30 Squadron fliers didn't know whether to be amused or appalled. It was all a big contrast to 'Ace's egalitarian ideas of a Mess – no such silly nonsense and carry-on there …

Things were very different the previous August when the Japanese had attempted to take the Bay and its vital airfields. It had virtually been the enemy navy and marines running things at night, while by day the Australian army men and Kittyhawks pushed back every Japanese thrust. Ralph took photographs of the simple marker erected at the end of Turnbull Strip. A plaque on it read: *'In memory of the officers and men of the 7th and 18th Infantry Battalions who gave their lives in defending Turnbull Field. This marks the westernmost point of the Jap advance, Aug-Sept, '42. 85 unknown Jap marines lie buried here.'*

Late in July, Ralph and Don are among a Flight of eight Beaus attacking the Japanese airfield at Gasmata, on the south coast of New Britain. Clarrie Trebilcock, their new CO, leads them. The 22 Squadron Bostons have given the strip and installations a thorough pasting before the Beaufighters arrive, so the enemy is more than prepared when the Beaus and escorting Kittyhawk fighters come in. Clarrie is anxious to make a good impression, despite the lead in the air. Though aware of the Squadron maxim of only one run on a defended target, he goes around again after his first pass. As Clarrie's number two, Ralph has no choice but to follow his leader down for a second time. The two aircraft are diving on the radio and radar hut when Don calls to Ralph: "Ack-ack – tracking on our tail and gettin' closer!" But Clarrie is still diving, and Ralph has to stay with him. The little black fragments are very near when one of the Kittyhawks passes them in an even steeper dive. He opens up on the Japanese gun. It stops shooting.

"Thank our lucky stars for that 'Kitty' bloke!" breathes Don after they'd completed the strafe and are following Clarrie home. "That Jap would've had us as sure as God made little apples!"

Poor Gary Hunter didn't get off quite so lightly on this strike. He brought his Beau back to Milne Bay with two feet of its port wingtip shot away and decided he'd need extra approach speed in case he stalled. But he was still airborne halfway along the strip and only touched down well past the Duty Pilot's tower. With the end of the runway – and the river – rushing at him, Gary applied full brake and ground-looped to avoid an overshoot. The Beaufighter turned two or three full circles and stopped. A very shaken pilot and navigator emerged, with only minor damage to the aircraft. Gary never got over the incident. As it was he'd only had about 250 hours in Beaufighters before his posting to the Squadron. Perhaps it wasn't enough – but on subsequent strikes, something always seemed to 'go wrong' with one system or another on Gary's machine and he'd break off the sortie. He was sent back south before his full tour time was up.

8

RIDING TO SLEEP

By August, 30 Squadron – its Moresby party and the aircraft and crews from Milne Bay – was established on Goodenough Island. This was the most northerly of three large islands directly south of enemy-held New Britain. Goodenough had previously been a Japanese base of operations, wrested from them as momentum fell to the Allies. The island was 21 miles in diameter with six tall peaks at its thickly wooded centre. The largest of these was Mount Vineuo, 8,000 feet high. Towards the eastern shore Mount Havaila, Modowa to the locals, sloped down to a three-mile wide coastal plain of coral reef at Bola Bola Bay. It was on this plain that US engineers had constructed Vivigani Strip from crushed coral. The airmen and groundstaff of 30 Squadron, along with their brethren in 22 Squadron and hundreds of other personnel, set up a large campsite on the lower slopes of Havaila. Clearings were hacked in the elephant grass, tents and flies were pitched and an Ops Room and Mess constructed. The war kept going.

The need to maintain maximum pressure on the Japanese was keenly felt. Because dispersal bays for the Beaufighters were still being bulldozed and Servicing Flight hadn't been able to complete its workshop, there were inevitable delays. At last an armed recce was planned for August 11th. It would be a pre-dawn take-off for three aircraft including those of Ralph and Bill. Bill's own plane, the one with his now widely-known Richmond Tiger on its nose, was grounded getting a sheared tail pin replaced, which annoyed him. Another kite was organised and after their lantern-lit breakfast and allocation of 'chutes and Mae Wests, the men clambered into the ute for their short trip to dispersal. The moon was down and only a few stars glimmered between thick clouds. Checks were made, engines run up and tested and the three dark bulks began their taxi to the flare path. Their Flight Leader was first away, gathering speed quickly and easing up well before the end of the flares. Ralph and Don were next to go. They hadn't done many night take-offs, but after Milne Bay and the rain, this was a relative cakewalk. Everyone had been briefed about the problem of Fergusson Island on a night take-off over the sea. As an aircraft lifted and left the flare path the black mass of the nearby island obliterated all horizon. If the pilot didn't go straight onto instruments he could easily get into too steep a nose attitude and stall. *"Use* that bloody artificial horizon in your kites," Trebilcock had insisted and Ralph made a careful note of the order.

His take-off and separation went to plan and as the flare path slipped away Ralph kept a careful eye on his instruments, bringing the Beaufighter into a gradual climb. Don was giving a heading as Ralph raised the cart, then their Flight Leader's radio call crackled: "L for Larry, K for Katie – this is Q for Queenie. All okay?"

"L for Larry – off deck and climbing. Heading 015. Over"

No reply from Bill. Their Leader called again – still no response.

"Either his radio's playing up or he's had problems on the ground," radioed the Leader. "We'll find out later. For now, let's get this recce out of the way." They made landfall on the enemy coast at dawn and thoroughly reconnoitered Gasmata and its approaches from Cape Beechey. Three and a half hours later, the two Beaufighters were back at Goodenough.

As Ralph jumped from his belly ladder at dispersal, he knew immediately that something had happened. Bert, their chief rigger, was kicking at the coral and muttering as Ralph approached. "It's Tassie, Ralph. 'E – 'e's bought it. Went into the sea on 'is take-off. George saw the wreck in shallow water off the anchorage this mornin'. We got out to it. Bill's dead. No sign of Bernie …" Cold sweat broke out on Ralph's forehead and he grabbed the undercarriage yoke for support. He gaped at Don, who was looking similarly pale and helpless.

"For God's sake," croaked Ralph, "all Tassie wanted was to see out the war and get back to Ruby and their kid. Who'd've thought …?"

"I'm sorry mate. God, I'm sorry," said Don.

Bill's body was brought in from the cockpit of his shattered aeroplane and prepared for burial that day. With the exception of a few crews on an afternoon patrol, every airman and groundstaff of 30 Squadron attended a funeral parade in the small cemetery at the foot of Mount Havaila. Wing Commander Trebilcock read the eulogy. Of course, he'd only known Bill for a relatively brief time but in those few weeks the outgoing Richmond Tiger had made a huge impression. Clarrie would have to break the news to Ruby Tassicker. Sometimes the job of a CO wasn't all it was cracked up to be, not by a long chalk.

When they looked closely at the wreckage of Bill's plane in its shallow water grave some of the men noticed the airscrews were in coarse pitch. If Bill had taken off with them in that setting, a rapid increase in nose attitude would have made a stall unavoidable. On the other hand impact with the sea could well have jolted the props from full fine to coarse setting. They would never know, just as Bill and Bernie, in the enveloping blackness, wouldn't have had any warning until ….

Sitting in the Mess, Bob took another swig of tea from his enamel mug. "Yeah, Ralph – I always thought Bill was unstoppable – larger than life, you know? Hell, if it can happen to him …"

"I know what you're getting at, Bob," replied Ralph. "Tends to put the wind up you a bit, doesn't it? If it's not the Japs it's a ruddy accident – or you get a dose of malaria or a cut on the coral that can knock you for a six. Maybe we've been up here too long, eh?"

"You've got a point there, Ralph. Since they've extended a tour from six months to nine months there's talk about making it twelve months. Hell's bells!"

Then Bob received the news from home. From their Berri fruit block his father wrote that Mrs Scott was very sick. It was a cancer, and there was little the local doctor or anyone else could do. Was Bob able to come home at this dark time? Mr Scott asked. Flying Officer Scott folded the letter slowly and carefully. He regarded his sombre reflection in the small shaving-mirror on its packing-case table in the tent and frowned. But he had to try at least. Bob changed into a fresh khaki shirt, put on his best pair of trousers and combed his hair. Donning and adjusting his cap to its optimum angle, he picked up the letter and went outside. It was mid-morning, just after the post had arrived, and he knew the CO would probably be in.

"Come in," came Trebilcock's reply when Bob knocked on the pole of his CO's tent. Bob entered and quickly laid out the situation for the Wing Commander, who contemplatively sucked on his pipe stem the whole while.

"Hmmm. A pretty sticky wicket, Bob," said Trebilcock. "If we can get you south – even for a short time – it might be a good thing. I'll check with Flight Lieutenant Warnes to see if we've got any kites scheduled for maintenance back home. As soon as one's available I'll let you know. If we can then tee up a fortnight's compassionate leave – how would that suit you?"

"I'd be very grateful, sir!" replied Bob. "Might be the – the last time I'll see my mother. Th-thank you very much."

"Don't mention it, Bob. If ever anyone's earned a spot of leave, you have. Been up here since October last year, is that right?"

"Yes sir. Sometimes it seems like just a couple of months – other times it's like ten years!"

"I can appreciate that," said Trebilcock. "All right, as soon as we've got a spare kite I'll organise you to take her down. Let's hope it won't be long."

As it turned out, Les Rawlinson's plane was found with white metal in a motor and they decided to replace the aircraft with one of the new Beaus then being assembled at Laverton. The CO put Bob down to be its pilot – for the first time in ten months, the young airman set off for his homeland. He flew with Phil via Ward's to Townsville and on to Laverton. Phil would stay there for the fortnight. Bob caught a ferry flight to Mildura's RAAF 'drome then boarded a bus for Berri.

As the battered vehicle rolled away the last few miles to his Riverland hometown, Bob found himself wondering more and more how he and his family would cope at this reunion. Letters invariably left out more than they revealed and Mum and Dad were pretty reticent at the best of times. The worst of it was that there was nothing he could do to change things, to alleviate pain and sorrow, to heal … And Bob had seen too much of death to have any illusions about peaceful passing away.

The bus was slowing at the bend by the two giant redgums, the rusty strands of fence and the old pepper tree cluster. There was the gate, the fussing chooks, the dogs – and, on the verandah of their home, a small figure looking up from a rocking chair. Bob thanked the driver, who was new on the run and clattered down the bus steps with his kitbag. He found himself hauling open the gate, shutting it automatically behind him and charging up to the person on the seat. "Mum!" he whispered, dropping his kit and falling to his knees to hug the woman. Who was murmuring, in her turn, as she wrapped thin, sun-browned arms around her son, "Bob! Oh,

Bob, it's wonderful to see you!" The kelpies went berserk with welcome, the hens quadrupled their clucking and Bob's fears about finding words to say evaporated as fast as a creek in summer.

"How are you, you old scallywag? Strewth, it's good to see you again! Nearly a year since I went north, eh? How's Dad and Betty and Ellie?" Bob had a hundred questions for his mother who simply smiled and grasped her son's hands and arms as best she could. Then Mrs Scott asked Bob to help her up ("I've been a bit shaky on the pins for the past few weeks, I'm afraid, dear.") and he gently lifted his mother from her chair.

Ellie heard the bus arrive and rattle away and came running from the shed. She jumped onto the verandah and flung herself at her brother. "Gidday, Bob! How's the airforce been treating you? Golly – you look almost yellow! Too many bananas?"

Bob laughed, one arm around his mother, the other hugging his sister. "Nah, you silly sheila – that's the atebrin. Stuff they give you to keep off malaria. And if you think *my* skin colour's crook, you should take a gander at the blokes who've had tinea treatment!"

Laughing and bantering to make up for too many intervening months, mother and children entered the house to put the kettle on and hear each other's news and gossip. Bob was profoundly grateful that he'd been given this opportunity. He could see without being told by his mother or sister how much the cancer had taken hold. Just make every moment count, old son, he told himself again and again as they chattered and reminisced between sips of tea. He couldn't help thinking of Ruby Tassicker, somewhere in Melbourne with young Madeleine – and no Bill. By God, these days're going to be precious, Bob reflected – for Mum and Dad and Ellie and Betty as well as for me. Just hope I can keep a stiff upper lip …

That wasn't too hard to manage but with only two weeks' leave and time galloping along, Bob looked to the moment of farewells with increasing trepidation. On the bright side, Dad seemed to be coping all right with the fruit block. Ellie was going to help with the summer picking and drying and they'd been promised assistance from the neighbour's young lads for the busy part of the season. Betty's job at the town grocery shop brought in some very useful shillings; the family was getting by.

Concerns and fears went both ways. Bob's family could never be as close to violent and continual death as the men in the Squadron. His parents and sisters knew well enough though, that war thrived on young lives. Too regularly the newspaper printed local names in its casualty lists. Bob's loved ones never ceased to be grateful that his name hadn't been among them; daily they prayed for his continued safety.

With just a few days of leave remaining Bob and Ellie found a quiet moment down by the mulberry canes and the irrigation channel at the back of the property. It was evening and coolness had dispelled the earlier heat of the day.

"Bob – I have to ask," Ellie suddenly said, "how much risk is there for you and your friends in the RAAF? Is the war dangerous where you are …?"

Bob paused, not quite sure how to answer. His favourite sister was always direct. Then he said: "Well, sis, it can get hot on the odd occasion – I won't spin you any yarn. But most of the time things're pretty humdrum. You almost find yourself looking forward to a sortie to let off steam. Compared with the AIF and militia blokes sloggin' up an' down ridges and through swamps and kunai, we've got it cushy and that's a fact!"

"But flying a plane – and in the tropical storms we hear about – with all those Zeros … And we know the Japs have been so cruel to men they've captured – "

"That's just part of the deal, Ellie. You don't think about it too much – it's all in a day's work. Heavens above – most of the time everyone's happy as Larry! The worst thing is the ruddy food they dish up. Fair dinkum, it makes a man want to see out the war down here and be spoiled rotten by Mum and you girls. Your cooking's just the ant's pants!"

Ellie laughed and hugged her brother. What he'd just told her would make the coming days and weeks a little easier. And if she could just – somehow – convince Mum and Dad and Betty as Bob had convinced her …

On the last day the whole family went into Berri to see Bob off. He would travel to Melbourne via Adelaide, meet up with Phil and ferry a new aeroplane to Goodenough. It had all been arranged. The war didn't forget you – or let you forget it – for long.

At the bus depot they got out of the venerable Essex. Bob pulled his kitbag from the boot and the Scott family began their goodbyes. Was there new greyness in Dad's thick moustache, a few more lines on the leathery face beneath the shapeless felt hat? Bob asked himself as he shook hands with his father. Then big embraces and moist-eyed grins from Ellie and Betty. Bob had satisfied himself that the girls were making things as easy as possible for their mother, not that he'd ever had many worries on that score. And then Mum. They'd ensured that she had a seat at the bus depot; now Bob eased down beside her. He held the thin figure in his firm grip and looked into her tired, pale blue eyes.

"I wouldn't've missed this leave for quids, Mum," he said. "Dad an' the girls have been looking after you pretty well, I'm pleased to see. You'll be putting on a bit of condition before much longer, sure as eggs!"

Then the bus clanked around the corner and everyone knew it was time. Bob squeezed his mother as tightly as he dared. "Keep your chin up, eh?" he entreated, smoothing a loose strand of hair away from her forehead.

"You too, dear. We'll look forward to your next letter."

"Too right – soon's I'm back on the island. Goodbye! 'Bye, Dad! 'Bye, girls!" And Bob Scott boarded the bus for Adelaide. He waved to his family through the dusty windowpane as the ancient engine juddered through its gear changes. The family waved back and the little tableau outside the Berri depot gradually grew smaller. They were still waving as the bus turned the corner of the main street.

9

UNDER THE SIMPLE STARS

U p in the South West Pacific Area war eddied and flooded, as insistent as ever. Its latest flux for 30 Squadron was barge hunting. After their Bismarck Sea debacle six months earlier, the enemy had resorted to small barges – 40 to 50 feet long – for supply and reinforcement of his New Guinea army units. Either towed or under their own power, these barges moved laboriously along the New Britain coasts by night and sought shelter in protected inlets or creeks during the day. The Japanese were masters of camouflage and it became a continuing challenge to spot them. Thirty Squadron's job was to sink the barges. If they were so anchored that an attack could not be made, the hunters noted their location to enable another sortie to deal with them further along the coast.

While Bob and Phil were down south several crews reported a particularly nasty surprise in Pal Mal Plantation, sited at Jacquinot Bay on New Britain's south coast. Intelligence knew that this was a staging point for the barges. To protect barge traffic the enemy had installed a very accurate ack-ack gun at Pal Mal. It made any recce or attack potentially lethal for 30 Squadron aircraft. Tony Robinson and Jim Cook dubbed the Japanese gunner 'Dead Eye Dick'. They'd been barge hunting one day along the Bay when they heard a loud crack and were narrowly missed by a shell fired by their new nemesis. The men left the scene quick smart – soon everyone marked the area as a 'hot spot'.

One day in early September, two Beaufighters flew a barge sweep combined with a recco of the Japanese road being built along that part of New Britain. In one Beau was an Army Liaison Officer, Captain Tom Gillies, with orders to make a detailed report on the state of the road. Gillies' pilot was Joe Newson, his navigator Rod Binns. The second Beaufighter on the sortie was piloted by Arch Thomas, navigator Pete Black. They reconnoitered road construction work between Cape Archway and Gasmata then flew along the coast on a now routine barge-sweep, heading east towards Jacquinot Bay. Following standard procedure for a hunt, Newson and Binns flew about 40 feet above the water, several hundred yards out from the shoreline. A few hundred yards astern and 1,000 feet above the sea Thomas and Black kept station, watching for bandits. Five pairs of eyes scanned every nook and fissure of the enemy coast for signs of hidden barges.

Before take-off from Goodenough that morning, the two crews had conducted a happy ceremony. It was Joe and Rod's last sortie before end of their tour and posting home. Later, Arch and Pete recalled what Joe said at the meal: "I want to make this last job one to remember."

The two aircraft approached Jacquinot Bay. Both crews were acutely aware of 'Dead Eye Dick' and his gun and had been briefed to keep well clear. Arch and Pete were therefore startled to see Joe closing on the coast, right at the little headland where the ack-ack gun was hidden among coconut palms.

"Crikey – he's looking for the gun!" says Thomas to his navigator.

"And the silly coot might just find it, too!" replies Black.

At that moment, the two men see Joe's aircraft diving at the point, with flashes of cannon and machine-gun fire from nose and leading edges of the Beau. Then Joe pulls out of the dive – but is that smoke coming from his starboard motor?

"'E's copped one!" calls Thomas on the intercom, and immediately radios Newson. "Electric Blue One – this is Electric Blue Two. How are you?"

"Electric Blue Two – we're okay. Kite's taken a hit from ack-ack. Starboard motor's gone. Am heading for home," buzzes Joe's reply.

"Roger. We're formating on you, Electric One. Maintain as much altitude as you can."

All four airmen know that a Beau on one engine cannot stay up for long. The airscrews on the Mark 1-Cs don't feather and the extra drag from a windmilling prop means that height gradually bleeds away. Only one direction then.

Ten nautical miles off New Britain, on track for Goodenough, Joe and Rod ditch. Luckily the sea is calm and the nose stays up on flare. Anxiously, their companions circle above.

"I can see 'em!" calls Black to his pilot as three figures scramble from front and rear hatches of the aircraft in the sea.

"They didn't waste time," replies Thomas. "And a good thing, too – the crate's just about gone."

"No sign of their dinghy," says the navigator as they maintain a circle above. "They might not've had time to get the thing out."

"Take a fix on their position. We're going to need it to have any show of rescuing 'em."

Pete makes the necessary calculations and Arch radios a brief Mayday to Goodenough. Below, three small figures in Mae Wests float on the vast expanse of the Solomon Sea. Their Beau has long since vanished. They are less than a dozen miles off the enemy coast. Thomas and Black circle a final time, dive over the tiny heads below and with a waggle of wings head for home at maximum cruise speed.

The bad news had spread quickly before Arch and Pete's return to Vivigani. First the Squadron tried the Americans. Could a PT boat, escorted by Beaufighters, rescue the downed men? "Sorry," said the Yanks, "too close to the enemy coast and on the far end of our range. No can do."

"God rot the Yanks!" said Wing Commander Trebilcock when he heard. "Have to do the best we can ourselves until an air-sea rescue's available. I'll want an aircraft there as soon as possible – with a dinghy and supplies. Those poor bastards've been in the sea since this morning. We've *got* to give 'em a fighting chance!"

Ralph and Don, as older hands in the Squadron, were asked to fly this sortie. Supplies were rapidly stowed aboard their plane for dropping to the downed men. The cargo included food, fresh water, flares, and – vitally – an inflatable rubber dinghy. Even in the tropics prolonged exposure in the sea was dangerous, not to mention sharks …

" Only ten miles from the Japs – they *have* to be picked up soon, no two ways about it," said the CO to the rescuers as their aircraft loaded the final items.

At 2200 hours, Ralph and Don took off from Vivigani Strip. The night sky was overcast and starless – Don would have to be spot-on with his fix on the last known position of the ditched Beaufighter. To make matters more difficult, another crew had taken their machine on a job the previous day. The compasses had gone out of alignment, as always happened when cannons were fired. There had been no time to 'swing' the aircraft to adjust the essential instruments.

But within an hour and a half they were near Jacquinot Bay. The plan was to drop parachute flares from Don's hatch in the belly of his cockpit. Risk of fire inside their plane made it dangerous to operate the device by hand, so a long cord was tied to each trigger. This would activate the flare when it was well clear of the aircraft.

"We're here, Ralph!" calls Don on the intercom.

"Okay – see if you can get that hatch open," replies Ralph. "Just hope the poor blighters are still somewhere down there."

Ralph throttles back and sets full flap. In the inky blackness, Don heaves open his hatch against the blasting roar of airflow. He hurls out the flare, gripping the end of its cord as he does. The long cylinder drops. The cord snaps. No light.

"Damn!" yells Don. "I'll have to try again, Ralph. Bloody thing didn't go off …"

"Okay – I'll turn," says Ralph, and brings the Beau onto its reciprocal heading. Don tries the remaining flare. The cord breaks again. The useless object plunges into the sea beneath.

"Bugger the thing!" says Ralph when Don tells him. "Now all we can try are our landing lights – they'll at least know someone's in the vicinity. We haven't Buckley's of spotting 'em ourselves."

Ralph and Don fly for the next hour in a parallel track search pattern up and down that section of coast, desperately hoping their friends in the water can see or hear them. The dinghy stays in the well behind Ralph. There is no point in dropping it.

"Fuel's getting low," Ralph calls to Don after another hour flying the grid pattern. "Better work out a heading on Gasmata for a leg to Goodenough."

"Okay. Let's hope they at least heard us. Might give 'em a bit of a boost until morning."

Don uses the astro compass to plot a course back to Goodenough; soon they are tracking for Gasmata, westward on New Britain's coast. Halfway there Ralph spots the first thunderhead, directly in their path.

"I'm not going to risk getting into that stuff, Don. We'll have to deviate. Do the best you can with best track and heading."

Both men know that the chances of entering a cu-nim and coming out the other side in one piece are small. Many airmen had tried, and too few lived to tell about it. Diverting from their planned course, Ralph has to repeat the procedure several times as the storm worsens. Every thirty seconds it seems, the obsidian sky is riven by crooked streaks of light. The crackling air around buffets their machine as if determined that the sea will claim another victim.

"This bloody storm's going to mess up ETA for our track to Goodenough!" calls Don. "And of course they'll be keeping a full blackout on the strip – we won't see any lights."

"Do the best you can, Don," responds Ralph, grimly monitoring the fuel gauges. He is furiously calculating: take-off at 2200 hours. Now 0330. How much left in the tanks? Crikey – will we end up ditching too? Fat lot of good that'd be!

"Don – I'm going to head for that cloud bank to port. It'll give us a reference. The New Guinea coast *has* to be somewhere that way." Soon after, behind the cloud, Ralph spies the thin dark curve of Bartle Bay on the New Guinea mainland. He now knows they are south of Goodenough, down towards Milne Bay, so he turns northeast. The gauge for their last tanks shows close to nil. Then Don is on the intercom: "Ralph – I can see a light ahead – about two o'clock!"

Immediately Ralph calls base, using the codewords 'Ginger-Blackout'. Never has a reply been so welcome or reassuring. In seconds, it seems, the strip ahead is re-illuminated by the flarepath and they have an aiming point. Then it is easy – an uneventful landing and up to the Ops Room to report. The next move has to be planned without delay.

At dawn, other Beaufighters fly to the location of the missing crew. Daylight brings luck – the three men are sighted and dinghies and supplies dropped without a hitch. The elated Beau crews circling above see the men wave and climb into the dinghies. But how to pick them up?

By this time the air-sea rescue Seagull kept at Kiriwina Island has arrived at Goodenough. Quickly Trebilcock arranges for his own navigator to fly with the Seagull pilot to pick up the men. The weather has worsened. The same front that Ralph and Don flew through has whipped up near gale conditions over the Solomon Sea.

On the morning of the third day, the Seagull floatplane takes off, heading for Jacquinot Bay into a heavy overcast. When the pilot doesn't call in on schedule for his return leg the men at Goodenough begin to worry. Two hours after ETA – still no word. Two Beaus are sent out to investigate and return later that afternoon to report no sign of the Seagull but that Newson, Binns and Gillies, in their life-rafts, are drifting towards the New Britain coast. Back to square one. There is no more gen on the Seagull. Either the weather or the Japs have accounted for them, poor devils.

The next day another Beaufighter flies out to the three men, dropping more supplies as well as messages of cheer from their comrades. The day after that, bad news. The two empty dinghies are sighted on a beach near Cape Cunningham. No sign of the men. New Britain coastwatchers can provide no other clues. Now the Squadron fears the worst – that the three are in enemy hands. Then it will be one of two options: POWs at Rabaul, or execution. Even before the Bismarck Sea Battle, the Japanese had shown little mercy to captured airmen – afterwards – well, the chances of being spared are slim, to say the least. A summary execution by bayoneting or beheading is more than 'on the cards'.

"You wouldn't read about it," said Ralph to Bob and Don in the Mess. "It was their last job before posting home – poor sods!"

"Yeah. And Arch reckoned they deliberately tried to knock off 'Dead Eye Dick'," commented Don.

"Except he got in first," said Bob.

There was little else to add. Only the last, excruciatingly difficult letters for Wing Commander Trebilcock to write to the men's relatives with the usual military terminology: 'Missing in Action' and 'Possibly a POW' … How flimsy and desperate that 'possibly' really was every man in 30 Squadron well knew. And each man was also starkly aware that it might be his turn on the next op.

Eight days later, the new name on that lengthening list was Clarrie Trebilcock himself. A flight of three aircraft led by the CO was strafing barges and supply dumps at Cape Hoskins when the Wing Commander's Beau caught a burst of ack-ack. In the other two machines, the horrified crews heard Trebilcock's final words, spoken to his navigator: "Come up front, laddie – I've been hit …" Then their Beaufighter simply nosed into the sea. The impact must have killed pilot and navigator in an instant.

The replacement CO would have to write the requisite letters and official report. For Squadron Leader Barry Bolt, it was a hard induction into his new role in 30 Squadron.

10

FOREVER FLED

Thirty Squadron desperately needed a fillip for its sagging morale. Early in October two Beau crews were flying a barge sweep near New Britain when they spotted an unescorted Betty. The Japanese pilot was in trouble and he knew it. He dived his comparatively sluggish machine to sea level at full throttle but the two RAAF aeroplanes were quickly on its tail. First Johnny Marron's Beau put the enemy rear gunner out of action, allowing the second aircraft to close. At 200 yards, Arch Thomas opened fire for the kill. The green-grey bomber caught alight, faltered in its flight path and hit the sea. There were no survivors. That night in the mess, precious beer flowed in celebratory quantities as the four victors – Marron, Gollan, Thomas and Black – were feted by their comrades.

Then the Rabaul raid. This was going to be a very big op. From MacArthur down, the shiny bums who planned it wanted to take the Treasury Islands and Bougainville by November. To assist their objective, shipping and airfields at Rabaul had to be 'neutralised', in official parlance.

"Rabaul!" snorted Ralph. "For crying out loud – that won't be any easy job, not by half!"

"Oh, I dunno," said Don as they watched the fitters down at dispersal. "I wouldn't mind a spot of action."

"We'd get plenty of that, all right – no fear. Is it *five* airfields the Japs've got there? And how many ack-ack guns? 350? 400?

"But it'll be a combined op, from what I've been hearing. A big one. They reckon we'd have dozens of Lightnings for top cover."

"And us on the deck – just sitting ducks for those Japs waiting on the ground. Not to mention the fighters they'll have up, for God's sake!"

"Ah, we can outrun their fastest kites, you know that, Ralph."

"So far, yes … so far. How long does our luck hold? This'd be our first strike on Rabaul – let's hope it won't be our last one, full stop! To tell you the honest truth, Don, I'm not too comfortable with this job."

Too clearly did Ralph remember Bill and Bernie, Jack and Sandy, 'Grumpy' Edgerton, Clarrie Trebilcock, Newson and Binns and Gillies. No one was immune; there were never any guarantees. Hell, what on earth was Don thinking? To *want* to be on a job like this one …

"Ah well, mate," said Don cheerfully, "they may give us a rest this time. Some of the new chums'll get the nod for sure, and we've had our share of ops lately, eh?"

"I hope you're right, Don. I don't want to get the wind up yet, at any rate."

As it turned out, Ralph and Don's names weren't on the Ops Board a day later. But Bob and Phil were down for the Rabaul strike – the CO needed a mix of old and fresh crews on this job. Men had to be 'blooded' all the time and veterans helped steady them in this difficult process.

Briefing was lengthy and detailed. Barry Bolt and the IO took participating crews through plans for the raid very carefully. They were to leave Goodenough at 0900 the next day to stage through Dobodura in New Guinea. They would rendezvous there with

Yank Mitchells and Lightnings. All up there would be 300 planes. The brass hats were taking it very seriously; their timetable was strict and had to be kept to. If the attackers didn't arrive over target together the Japanese would have a field day.

So the men and machines of 9 Ops Group prepared. Fuelled and armed, checked and tissied up with as much TLC as fitters, riggers and armourers could bestow, the Beaufighters and Bostons were readied for their strike. The groundstaff boys of both 30 and 22 Squadrons wanted to give their respective aircrews every possible chance to get to Rabaul and back. They all knew about bloody Murphy and his merciless maxim: if it can go wrong, it will … SNAFU, TARFU, FUBAR or FUBB – anything could happen.

In the humid darkness of their tent the night before their trip to Dobadura, Bob and Phil talked about the 'Rabaul Show'.

"Jeez – this'll be the biggest stoush we've been in, eh, Bob? What're our chances of getting away with it?" Phil, like Ellie, was always to the point.

"I reckon it'll boil down to the element of surprise," answered Bob. "Just as long as every kite gets there at the same time and if the Japs don't have wind of our approach, we should get in and out okay."

Both men knew how much depended on tight security for all ops but this one took the cake. Briefings stressed and restressed 'no chat' about Rabaul. Information was issued strictly on an 'as needed' basis. Nevertheless – as usual – word got around, via the ubiquitous 'latrine-o-gram', bush telegraph and boredom-induced gossip about camp. A palpable air of anticipation and excitement spread quickly.

In the early morning of October 11th, Squadron Leader Bolt headed both Flights of 30 Squadron's planes. It totalled thirteen Beaus. More than a few crews regarded the number as unlucky. What might it portend? But in the half-light of semi-day, no one had time to dwell on omens. They went through checks and began taxiing from dispersal to the main runway. The 22 Squadron Bostons, bombed up, were first on the queue. Then Murphy struck. Bob had just completed his final checks and was waiting for the signal to go as a Boston commenced its take-off run on Vivigani Strip. Quite a few machines were already away, and this seemed to be one more uneventful exit from Goodenough. The Boston had almost reached separation speed when the nose-wheel of its tricycle undercarriage suddenly gave way. At full throttle, the aircraft's momentum drove its belly into the strip and the whole thing cartwheeled with a screech of rending and collapsing aluminium. It burst into flames in front of everyone's horrified stares. The crash siren wailed; figures began converging on the blazing wreckage. Every man desperately and silently screamed at the crew of the Boston to get out. Two crewmen scrambled from the gunner's compartment and dropped to the strip, but there was no sign of a third man. The flames took an even fiercer grip on the doomed bomber – evil black smoke billowed, bright flame gobbled voraciously. The siren's moan twisted everyone's nerves to snapping point. No one dared get close – the bomb load could go up at any moment – and who would have survived the flames anyway? Men nearer the blazing wreck then heard screams from its cockpit. The pilot was trapped and being cooked alive – and not a thing anyone could do. Bob gripped the control spectacles with clammy fists as sweat streamed down his forehead and neck.

"Christ Almighty, Phil! Christ Almighty!" was all he could utter, jerking out the syllables through teeth clenched tight.

"The poor bastard," groaned Phil. "What hope's 'e got?"

Both men knew the answer to that. But they were in the middle of the first stage of a strike. Soon one of the bulldozers and a crash truck were busy at the smouldering pieces of what had been an aeroplane, shoving and hauling blackened scraps to the edge of the strip. An order came for take-offs to resume; the attack on Rabaul must proceed on schedule.

For the remaining Beaus and Bostons, the flight to Dobodura went without further incident. They all knew about the Allied airfield they were heading for – briefing had been thorough and some crews were acquainted with 'Dobba' from previous trips. It's a hellhole, was the general opinion. In the highlands on the Samboga River, weather was appalling. The rain never stopped – Milne Bay without the Bay, some fellows said. Sodden, humid, malaria-ridden (the ruddy mozzies didn't let up) and surrounded by thick jungle – not an ideal place to run a war. Even the legs of a stretcher would sink in the moist mud – and that was on a dry day!

So when departure time neared the next morning the new arrivals were surprised to hear that *dust* might present problems for their aircraft.

"Yessir," drawled the USAAF Colonel at briefing, "that Goddamn dust'll build up even after a heavy rain. With our B-25s an' fighters leavin' first, you Aussies take care in that murk, okay?"

But it wasn't okay at all. Waiting in the marshalling area on a taxiway, Bob and Phil anxiously noted the increasing concentration of fine grey-brown dust behind the Mitchells and Lightnings as they thundered down Dobadura Strip. Haze blossomed and hung in the morning stillness above the airfield. As the last Lightning lifted off through the thick pall, orders came for the thirteen waiting Beau crews – they were to delay take-off. To attempt flying through it would invite a prang. Reasoning that the faster Beaufighters could catch up with the others before reaching target, the brass hats ordered 30 Squadron to hold.

Fifteen minutes later the haze had sufficiently dispersed and take-offs resumed. Every Beau got away all right but now time was not on their side. If they flew above cruising speed at this stage there might not be enough fuel left to manoeuvre, take evasive action over Rabaul and return. But if the Beaus got to target *after* the others the Nips would be fully alerted and have fighters up. Consequently, Squadron Leader Bolt took them to Rabaul at just above best cruise speed.

It wasn't enough. Ten minutes out from target things got hot. The leading Beaus sighted two Mitchell Squadrons and a group of escorting Lightnings heading towards them – on their way back from Rabaul. As they neared the Beaufighters, the lead Mitchells broke formation and opened up! Tracer flashed between Fred Catt and Chas Harris's planes and things looked even worse as the Lightnings prepared to attack.

But then Bolt was on the radio: "This is *Bolt aircraft!* I repeat, *Bolt aircraft! Stop firing!*"

The Yanks, to everyone's relief, got the message. They ceased shooting, re-formed and continued on track for 'Dobba'. Now the Beaus would have to press ahead alone to make their run on Tobera Airfield.

Intelligence had briefed the Squadron very well about Tobera. It was the newest Japanese strip at Rabaul with a 1,100 yard all-concrete runway and revetments for 75 fighters. The field was surrounded by well-concealed ack-ack sites, each one – as anyone who'd been to Rabaul knew – quite accurate.

They follow Bolt at treetop level a few nautical miles out from Tobera. It is on a ridge; they will have to fly up the slope to get to it. Close to full throttle the thirteen machines streak towards the crest. Then up and over spraying the strip and revetments and buildings with fire. The first ack-ack puffs appear, but before Bolt can even think of a second run the warning is on their radios: "*Bogeys –* above and coming in *fast!*" Nothing for it but to open taps to the maximum and dive for the sea a few miles to the southwest. Poor Chas Harris turns the wrong way and finds himself over *another* enemy strip with seemingly every ack-ack gun in Rabaul doing its utmost to get him.

But their main worry is the fighters. These are flown by Navy pilots, the best the Japanese have got, and they are angry! Most of the Beaus are out above the water now heading away with every rev they can muster. They hear Bolt call up from the van of the fleeing machines: "Home to mother!" No one feels much comforted.

Bob and Phil, in the rearguard of the escaping aircraft, are still over the jungle when Phil calls: "Bob! Bandit on Fred's tail – on our starboard beam – three o'clock!"

"Roger – let's see if we can help," replies Bob. He turns to starboard, climbing and aiming to get behind the enemy fighter. He is almost there and at extreme range of 800 yards tries a burst to scare the enemy pilot. But the Zeke is sticking to Fred. Suddenly, Phil on intercom again: "*Bob*! One closin'! *Break off – brea –* " Then the cannon shells ripping – mad clangs and bright explosions whipping around Bob's cockpit. No sound from Phil.

Bob bunts and rolls on Phil's warning, doing everything he can to get low. With oppo dead or unconscious he has no 'eyes' on the fighter. He has also rammed throttles through the gate. His dive is approaching 340 knots. VNE is not much above this.

Ahead, the coast and grey shining sea beckon the racing Beaufighter. Hot sweat pours into Bob's saturated uniform. Now he is near the deck well over VNE. He just has to … Suddenly the Beau jumps, shakes and flips into a half-roll. The jungle flashes up and, at full revs, Bob's aircraft plunges into the trees.

Twelve Beaufighters returned to Goodenough. Fred's oppo reported at de-brief that he'd seen Bob climbing to help them then had a fighter on his own tail which scored hits. After that, during Fred's evasive manoeuvres, he'd lost sight of Bob and Phil's plane.

"We can only assume they've bought it, then," said the IO slowly, frowning. "*No* top cover for you fellows – all because of that bloody cock-up at Dobodura!" McInnes had heard all about the dust problem there and the take-off delay. "Wouldn't it rock you? Wouldn't it just rock you …?"

All too soon, as news of the Rabaul fiasco spread, Ralph and Don learned what had happened. In the small Ops Room among its disconsolate group of airmen they looked at each other. Don spoke first.

"Jeez, Ralph – I remember telling you I wanted to be in on that job. Reckon you were right about luck runnin' out – not for us, but for poor Bob and Phil. First Tassie and Bernie, now … Will it be our turn to go west next?"

Ralph didn't tell Don that these had been exactly his own thoughts when he'd heard about their friends. Heavens above – how far Don and he had come since nearly a year ago! Those callow young men who'd been so keen to get into the fight. The big question of course – now they'd found out so much about the fight, which would come first – end of the war or end of them? When you got down to tin tacks, all the fine-sounding phrases – from Curtin to Blamey to MacArthur – boiled away to nothing. Just bumph which looked nice in newspaper headlines; good quotes for history books later. But in the final account, those at the sharp end had to cop it – and give it back – as best as they could, knowing all the while how putrid the real thing was.

Ralph thought a lot about Bob and Phil over the following days. Many times, avoiding company if he could, he headed down to the rushing flow which had its headwaters somewhere on the slopes of Havaila. As he floated and bumped in the cool cascade pouring over the waterfall just upstream, the Flying Officer daydreamed and pondered. If only this water could wash away fear as easily as it got rid of grime and insects, he thought to himself. There are days when I've just about had it. How long can a man keep going? Crikey, if I could give the whole bloody war away tomorrow I'd do it at the drop of a hat! Poor Bob and Phil. Poor, poor bastards …

No one in the Squadron, as far as Ralph knew, used words like 'sacrifice' and 'glorious death' any more. Probably the front line Jap soldier, for all the gen the Squadron got about Japanese fanaticism and devotion to the Emperor, was in the same boat. In the end you did what you had to do until your tour finished or you … Most of the men preferred to think of their return home. They all knew that the war was well on the way to being won. The objective now was to stay around long enough to see that day, and hope like hell you wouldn't be one of those poor devils making 'the supreme sacrifice' … Only people a long way from New Guinea made free with bullshit like that.

To help exorcise the depression which descended on 30 Squadron with Bob and Phil's deaths came its second victory. Intelligence reported a regular Japanese float-plane patrol in the Cape Cunningham-Cormoran Head vicinity, so a four-Beaufighter Flight was sent to intercept it. Late in the day of 23rd October, Ralph and Don were among the hunters who sighted a lone Jake off the coast at 1,000 feet. The enemy pilot spotted them at the same instant and dived for the sea. Ken Drury got on his tail, closed to 150 yards and directed four short bursts into the float-plane. It caught fire and plummeted into a hillside a mile west of Cape Orford. A few rounds from the enemy rear gunner caused minor damage to Ken's machine.

Ralph and Don, circling above, watched it all, from Ken's swoop to the pyre of smoke and flame from the wreckage on the hill.

Don said: "Strewth, Ralph – I wonder if that Jake crew had mothers and wives and kids back in Japan? They can't all be monsters like the papers make 'em out to be."

"I have thought about it, Don, I've got to admit. You mustn't let it get you down, though. At least they were fightin' Japs. Not like those poor swine in London and Hamburg and Berlin in the bomber war …"

Both men had seen and heard plenty of reports on the tit for tat RAF, USAAF and Luftwaffe raids in Europe, targeting civilians and with heavy losses on both sides. They'd heard many first-hand accounts of entire cities burnt out and in ruins. Ralph and Don knew that this was the first war in history to send such massed aerial ordnance deliberately against men, women and children. Would it be the last?

11

NOTHING I CARED

Then came November '43, and with it two races. One was to be run in far-away Melbourne at Flemington Racecourse. The other was much closer to home – in fact, at 30 Squadron's very own base of operations. Towards the end of the previous month, Bostons and Beaufighters were returning to Goodenough from a combined strike when a Boston got back to the strip several minutes ahead of the first Beau. The Boston boys began to brag about their kites' speed compared with the 'poor ol' Beaufighters …' Pride was at stake. Aiming to satisfy honour and prove a point once and for all, representatives from each squadron organised the Great Race. It would coincide with the Cup.

The Bostons were powered by twin Wright Cyclone radials and the latest Beaus on the island had Hercules XVIII motors. These were bigger powerplants than the Cyclones, but then the Bostons were much lighter than the Beaus. Overall, it seemed a fairly even proposition – except of course to the highly partisan men of the Squadrons. As Race Day neared, various odds and starting prices were on offer around Goodenough. With at least 1,000 US marines as well as 5,000 RAAF men on the island it amounted to quite a tote.

Stripping every ounce of excess weight from their chosen

aircraft, groundcrews readied them for the race with a will. All armament was taken out, gunports and fairings taped over, surfaces waxed and buffed till they glistened. In its zeal to improve the odds for their plane, the Boston crew removed the air induction scoops from each motor. Their efforts to reduce drag were to have a decisive influence upon the race!

On the afternoon of November 2nd, it was on. Squadron Leader Bolt flew the Beau for his Squadron; Wing Commander Townsend piloted 22 Squadron's gleaming Boston. Referee-observer was Wing Commander 'Woof' Barker of 76 Squadron, flying a Kittyhawk. 'Woof' would broadcast a running commentary on the race, relayed to the island over specially prepared loudspeakers.

Sixteen nautical miles out from the coast of Goodenough, the Ref ordered the start over his radio. The two 'mounts' were off. The Boston, reported 'Woof', jumped to an early lead. This was expected by pundits from both Squadrons – the bomber's quick acceleration always gave it an initial advantage. As its revs mounted however, the Beaufighter began to close the gap. At 305 knots, 'Woof's' Kittyhawk engine gave up the ghost. The men waiting back at Goodenough guffawed and cheered as they heard his final inventive-laced observations on his now cactus engine. 'Woof' would have to throttle right back and limp home to Vivigani. But the Ref wasn't the only one experiencing engine difficulties. A lengthening plume of black smoke poured from each motor of Townsend's Boston. Those missing induction scoops had reduced ram effect on the engines too much – at full revs the air-fuel ratio was too rich. Two more motors shot and the Beau an easy winner. The Boston backers reluctantly parted with their wager payments and immediately demanded a re-match. The war, however, intervened.

Next day they went on a combined op to Pal Mal, preserve of 'Dead Eye Dick'. As expected, the Beaus and Bostons encountered heavy ack-ack. Townsend's plane was hit and he ditched off the coast. Unlike poor Newson, Binns and Gillies, pilot and navigator reached shore undetected and spent the next twelve weeks evading Japanese capture with the help of friendly tribespeople. The 22 Squadron boys were overjoyed when the missing men got back. By this time though, both 30 and 22 Squadrons had moved base again.

Their new home was in the Trobriand Island group, 80 nautical miles north of Goodenough. Kiriwina, its main island, was flat and forested with palms, scrub and native gardens. Its composition was coral, the highest point only 80 feet above sea level – in contrast to Mount Havaila at Goodenough. The latest base had been meticulously prepared. It had two well-graded coral strips, revetments, supply-dumps, hospital, piped water supply and hundreds of tents – the whole huge agglomeration essential to fight and win a modern war. Newly-arrived aircrew quickly discovered that 'Kiriwina' meant 'island of beautiful women' and many (if not quite all) of the men had no difficulty conjuring up images of nubile, grass-skirted maidens lined up to greet them.

But fraternisation and 'R and R' were far from the war-planners' reasoning in scheduling this shift of ops. The whole war in the South West Pacific Area had now moved north, with the Japanese virtually finished in Papua and New Guinea. Here, their few remaining strongpoints were cut off, starved of supplies and ammo, disease-ridden and had become a shadow of their earlier fighting capability. They would simply be left, as MacArthur wryly stated, to 'wither on the vine'. The Generalissimo was intent to the point of obsession with setting foot once more in his beloved Philippines; after all, he had on several carefully stage-managed occasions vowed to return.

A big part of the Philippine push was to remove or reduce Rabaul as a major base of operations for the enemy. With its harbour and airfields isolated, Japanese replenishment of their New Guinea troops would be close to zero. Raid after raid was ordered on this strongpoint – Mitchells, Liberators, Fortresses, Marauders, Bostons, Beauforts, Catalinas and Venturas flew constant sorties, escorted by Lightnings, Kittyhawks, Thunderbolts, Spitfires and Beaufighters.

Kiriwina was much closer to Rabaul than Moresby or Goodenough so it provided a perfect stepping-off point. And with Allied naval and air superiority, the Japanese had little opportunity for mounting any serious counter attack on the new base. As most men had long agreed, the war was as good as won. It was now simply a matter of time – and of keeping in one piece – until then.

While the Beaus and Bostons were in transit to Kiriwina, 79 Spitfire Squadron had a 'kill' there. Ian Callister, just turned 21 and affectionately dubbed 'The Kid' by his comrades, was patrolling the northern approaches to the island with another Spit. He sighted what he thought might be a bogey, checked with the strip and received confirmation that the strange aircraft was indeed an intruder. Callister gave immediate chase with full boost on his Merlin engine and an inevitable tail of black exhaust streaming behind him across the blue Pacific sky. At 800 yards 'The Kid' fired his first burst. He saw pieces fly off the Japanese machine's mainplane and closed to 600 yards. Callister fired again and this time the target simply disintegrated. Once again the evening Mess filled with jubilant discords; in honour of his victory they asked the modest youngster to lead his Flight on Friday's Dawn Patrol.

At 0600 hours that day, in darkness, Ian got the green light from the Tower and taxied his Spit onto the strip. But then an awful SNAFU. At the same moment, 'Woof' Barker was landing a Kittyhawk. The two aircraft collided and caught fire in the middle of the runway. 'The Kid' was crushed in the splintered remnants of his cockpit. 'Woof', desperately throwing off his harness, extricated himself from the burning wreckage of his machine and rushed to the other man's aid. It was impossible to reach him. With his clothing alight, the Wing Commander rolled in the mud at the edge of the runway to douse the flames, refused medical help from the ambulance crew which had raced to the scene and calmly gave orders for the Dawn Patrol to resume with a new leader. Only then, in agony from his burns, did Barker allow the medics to get him to the hospital.

Under constant care from the dedicated MO and his staff, the Wingco began the first slow stages of healing. For many hours each day he was placed in an oil bath to soothe the shocking blisters on his body, drifting in and out of a morphia-induced haze.

After two weeks the MO felt that 'Woof' would be fit enough to endure the trip south for vital post-burns surgery so that damaged tissue could be restored. The Beaufighter Squadron was asked to supply a plane and men for the task – after all, they had shown they were fast! Squadron Leader Bolt wanted an experienced crew for the job – and gave the nod to Ralph and Don.

"You could both do with a spot of leave, in my book," said the CO to pilot and navigator in the Ops Room. "And this flight's going to require more than a tad of care. God help the poor blighter if you get into bad air or put her down heavily. Do you get my drift?" Ralph and Don certainly did, and went off soon after to draw up a flight plan, check the latest Met and collect supplies. They were to carry 'Woof' on a specially rigged stretcher slung in the well between pilot and navigator and also make room for two medics. These men would monitor the patient's condition and administer the mercy of morphine on their fraught journey.

On the morning of November 25th, the flight began. First, they gingerly raised 'Woof' into the well of their Beau via the belly-ladder. The medics made the Wingco as comfortable as possible in the far-from-ideal air ambulance. Ralph went through his pre-take-off checks and waited for the thumbs up from the chief medic.

A smooth take-off from Kiriwina's North Strip and an uneventful crossing of the Owen Stanleys by 0800 hours was followed by a relatively routine hop to Townsville. Here their Beau was refuelled with 'Woof' still strapped, uncomplaining, to his makeshift bed. Despite his agony the young officer was able to inform Ralph how much fuel and oil their kite had taken on. "You fellows're making this trip a piece of cake!" he grinned, though 'Woof's' cheery tone was often interrupted by spasms of pain. His pale, clammy face and gritted teeth conveyed much more than the man's carefully chosen words.

So to another careful take-off and on to Charleville. Don had hoped that from here, weather permitting, they would make Bankstown in one hop. But then the first gremlin. Almost as soon as Ralph had got their machine airborne and raised the cart, their radio and intercom went dead. No matter what Don tried, the damned thing wouldn't revive. The only substitutes were hand-scribbled notes, passed backwards and forwards via the medics between Ralph and Don. Next FUBAR came with the deteriorating weather; their horizon ahead was closing in. A quick decision was made after pilot and navigator discussed the situation on their message-pad – they would give away the plan of going straight to Bankstown. But Don, a native of Newcastle and its surrounding areas, had a good back-up strategy. He wrote to Ralph: "Turn through 111 degrees – fly down Hunter Valley – we'll hit Williamtown."

Don's suggestion was, in Squadron slang, 'just what the doctor ordered'. They reached Williamtown 'drome without further trouble, though 'Woof's' pain was screwing down tighter and tighter now. The promising news from the Williamtown Met was a cloud base of 3,000 feet and only light stream showers between there and Sydney. "You chaps should have a clear, straight run down the coast to Bankstown," predicted the Met Officer.

He was totally wrong. Not far south of Williamtown after take-off, their radio still malfunctioning, the airmen found the sky steadily darkening. Soon Ralph had no alternative but to descend to sea level, with heavy rain all around and the coast a faint grey sliver on their starboard. "Another FUBB!" wrote Don tersely. Through it all, the two Hercules motors kept up their deep, reassuring drone – if any kite was reliable in all weather, a Beau was.

The grey-out persisted all the way to Sydney, easing sufficiently for Ralph to join the special air corridor for the Sydney area. Then another note from Don: "To port – 10 degrees – it's the Mascot approach." Ralph thanked Don, took their aircraft a few degrees left and in minutes was on final to Bankstown aerodrome. They landed with hardly a bump.

As Ralph taxied towards the hangars he observed vehicles racing along the strip from the 'drome buildings. Willamtown had obviously phoned through for the Bankstown medical staff to be prepared for the special arrival. Just as well, thought Ralph – after twelve hours in this crate, even a man like Woof'd be at the end of his tether. Not surprisingly, as the medical boys lowered 'Woof' from the Beau into the ambulance, he yelled loudly and unashamedly. Another jab of 'morph' then off to the hospital for attention not available on a forward base in the South West Pacific.

After farewelling their passengers, Ralph and Don also parted. They arranged to meet at Laverton at the end of the fortnight for return to Kiriwina. Don planned to visit his parents at Newcastle. Ralph would make for Adelaide with a similar goal.

Two days later, thanks to RAAF Courier and the train service, Ralph Raymond was back at Glenelg and the home he'd left so long – years it seemed – before. Mr and Mrs Raymond, Beryl and young Alf were over the proverbial moon to have their hero back.

"Oh, Ralph – you look taller and slimmer! And that natty navy-blue uniform suits you to a 'T'," bubbled eighteen year-old Beryl after they'd all hugged and kissed. His parents simply stood back and beamed in their love and pride and deep gratitude to see their son again.

"How many medals have you got, Ralph?" Alf burst in excitedly. "I've told me mates at school that you'll have lots after a year in New Guinea." Alf was only twelve, and was even more taken in by patriotic hyperbole than his peers and so many of his elders.

"Sorry, Alf," Ralph chuckled, "no gongs for your big brother. They're not giving the things away – not yet, at any rate!" And everyone joined in the laughter.

But like Bob Scott's family six months earlier, the Raymonds nurtured deep concern and fears for their young airforce pilot. Not even Alf was ignorant of the casualty statistics regularly appearing. Although things seemed to have now definitely turned in the Allies' favour, no quick victory was yet in sight. There would have to be many more deaths before it was finally finished.

The next day the family and some close friends sat on steamer chairs on the smooth couch grass of the Raymonds' tennis court. With cool drinks and nibbles in the early December sun, the war and all its baggage seemed very distant. As he took in the 'pok pok' of gut on tennis ball, the lilting, amazingly musical pitch of the female register and streams of chatter and laughter from various youngsters, Ralph felt civilization happily moving him far away from the front. Old Buster, their big woolly Airedale, seemed quite amenable to this state of affairs. He laid his shaggy head contentedly on Ralph's tennis shoes as the family sipped tea in the shade of the pepper tree. How different this all was to the tropics, where sun hit harshly on the white coral strips, where sago palm, kunai and elephant grass burned vivid green against the sky and where the roar of aero engines and deep voices from hundreds of male bodies formed the daily chorus.

The best news, Ralph reflected, was that his tour time had very nearly expired. Even though the powers that be had extended the initial six months to twelve, then offered earlier crews a second tour, he realised there was every likelihood he would see out the war in Test and Ferry Flight. Or, he thought, I could go back to instructing – though God knows *that* has its moments …

"Yes – there's a good chance I'll make it," the young man murmured aloud, but only to himself.

Ralph's thought chain was broken then by a loud and jocular altercation over a decision in the tennis match – in or out? With each pair in the mixed doubles stoutly maintaining its side of the issue, the point was replayed in good humour. The game, and life away from war, continued.

Over the next few days, feeling increasingly spoiled by his family, Ralph made time to look up as many of his old companions as possible. In the front bar of the Pier Hotel he organised a beer or two (and an excellent brew – not like the bottled stuff on Kiriwina!) with several of the old lacrosse team. Max Wauchope, Ron Roach, Fred Stone and he raised a pint glass each and someone said: "To the end of the ruddy war!" Which all present echoed with a lusty: "Hear, hear!"

Max, in a reserved occupation, had often wondered about the fighting. Though content not to be ducking bullets or firing them he carried a healthy admiration, even adulation, for those who had done so, who had to keep doing so. During their second round he asked Ralph outright: "Up in New Guinea, cobber – d'you have – are there many close shaves for you blokes …?"

Ralph was caught on the hop, cold beer glass in one hand, 'Craven A' in the other. "Hell's bells, Max – it certainly has its moments! You just take it one day at a time – no long-term plans. I've had the wind up on quite a few occasions. And I'm always a happy chappy when we roll into dispersal after a job, let me tell you!"

Ron had come back, invalided, from Crete with the 6th Division. He'd undergone the same interrogation from their mate. Now he spoke. "Fair go, Max – the poor bastard wants to forget about the shooting for a day or two. Here you are draggin' it all up again for 'im!"

"It's all right, Ron," smiled Ralph. "If I put it too far to the back of my mind it'll be that much harder to cope with when this leave's up. But one thing, Max," he added, gazing levelly into his friend's eager eyes, "you mustn't believe ninety percent of the stuff in the newspapers. They're all peddling a doctored version of the real thing. Of course, it'd be hard to drum up support for a dinky-di war effort if people back here ever got a whiff of the real gen. Crikey, if even half of what the front line serviceman sees made it to the papers, the war'd be over and done with in a week!"

"Too true, mate!" said Ron. "What they printed about the Crete show gave the impression we'd knocked the stuffin' out of the Jerries – instead of the other way 'round. Newspapers – bulldust!" He shook his head vigorously and took a large swig of his pint. And Max had to leave it at that. All he would ever have to judge war by would be press reports, the wireless and the newsreels. Men who were closer wouldn't – or couldn't – convey its harsher, far more complex verities …

Ralph stumbled back home late that afternoon and decided to write a few letters then rest. The Adelaide summer was as benevolent as ever. Outside, Alf romped with Buster and their mother was pegging the weekly washing on the line. Dad was back at his Insurance Company. Life, banal and ordinary, went on. Ralph mused that this was just as he preferred it – no fuss, no 'conquering hero' nonsense. Heavens above, better leave that for a poor posthumous VC winner like Bill Newton. Bill's mates in 22 Squadron said that he never jinked – just flew straight in at a target to drop his bombs. He'd been shot down at Salamaua earlier that year. The Japs had captured him and chopped off his head with one of their samurai swords.

"The heroes – whatever the word means – good luck to 'em," said Ralph to the ceiling above the bed on which he'd sprawled. "I just want to come back in one piece an' if I can do it without letting anyone down, that'll suit me fine."

Now that he was thinking about the war again, Ralph realised that he had long since ceased to be concerned with abstractions like 'freedom versus fascism' and 'the Mother Country' and 'the Australian way of life.' Instead, it suddenly struck him, he was fighting for the men he'd become as close to as a brother – living and dead. For Don and Bill and Bernie, for Bob and Phil, and – of course – for 30 Squadron itself. Perhaps it sounded trite, but it was true. Kiriwina and the islands were the world he had come to know more intimately and completely than the sheltered inlets of little Adelaide. Was it really just over a year ago he'd left?

Even with his own family, during those last precious days of leave, Ralph found that he could speak only in the most general terms about the fighting. The trivia of camp life in the tropics; the hi-jinks he and his Squadron friends got up to; the terrible food – all were discussed in witty detail and ribald humour. Ralph never mentioned the crippling fear which now soaked through him before, during and after every sortie. Nor the dreams. Far better not to let on about the dreams … Not only for the sake of those he loved and desired to spare. Such visions were simply too close to the bone. They threatened – if unchecked – to tip him from control to a place from which he would be unable to exert control. The war, as it inevitably did for anyone who'd known it for long, engendered an incipient madness in him. Ralph feared this infiltrating darkness, feared it perhaps more than violent death itself. That would be the challenge, he knew, from now until the end – to stave off 'long long' – crack up and collapse. 'Keep on keeping on', his father jocularly exhorted in pre-war days. And Ralph remembered what he himself had said to Max about taking things 'one day at a time' up north. Yes, that was part of the answer. A large part.

A few days after that, the farewells had to be said, the last fond embraces and kisses and quiet tears between the Raymond family and their firstborn. Over the next weeks, Ralph would grasp the memory of that time as firmly as he'd hugged his mother, sister and brother and returned his father's handshake. Small but priceless drops of sustenance for a bone-weary spirit.

12

THAT TIME ALLOWS

At Laverton, Ralph met up again with Don and they set about cadging a lift on a courier flight heading north. Don had enjoyed his leave, but like Ralph, found it tantalisingly fleeting.

Before long the Solomon Sea and the tropics welcomed them back. Through the window of their C-47 the men spied the flat green and white splotch of Kiriwina on the turquoise ocean below.

"Our home away from home, eh, Ralph?" commented Don ironically as the Dakota joined circuit for the North Strip.

"You've got it in one, Don!" replied Ralph. "Can't wait till it finally *is* 'away' – for keeps!" And they registered with approval a good approach and landing by their pilot, then watched the blur of coconut palms get slower as the Dakota moved onto the taxiway. Back in the war – but how much, now, was the war back in them?

One week before Christmas, Ralph and Don got some indication. While they were down south a different maintenance system had been introduced by an Engineering Officer keen to make his mark on Servicing Flight. The new schedule abandoned the previous set-up of one crew – fitter, rigger and armourer – for each Beaufighter. Instead, rotating shifts of groundstaff would now work on a number of aircraft on a roster basis. The old ground crews split up between six to a dozen kites doing 80 hourlies, 40 hourlies and daily inspections. Cracks in the scheme soon appeared.

Ralph and Don, flying their first op since getting back, were taking part in a strike on Cape Gloucester. The three other Beaus had made their first run and Ralph lined up on the target – huts and dumps near the Gloucester strip. The buildings filled his reflector sight; he pressed the button. Nothing. At full revs, Ralph pulled up, banked and swore simultaneously. "You wouldn't read about it, Don!" he barked on the intercom. "Guns are U/S. Not one bloody squeak!"

Don gave a pithy rejoinder while Ralph followed the Flight around for a second run. Again, not a peep from either his cannons or machine-guns. Never had Ralph or Don felt so utterly vulnerable and impotent. They couldn't even report the weapon malfunction to their Flight leader under their radio silence regime.

Back at Kiriwina, Ralph let rip. He'd landed with the others and as he moved his Beau into dispersal he hurled open the top hatch, stood on the seat and furiously waved the EE/77 form to all and sundry. "Who on earth signed this flamin' thing to say my kite was fully serviceable? Serviceable, my Aunt Fanny!"

The upshot of it all was that, a few days after Squadron Leader Bolt heard about the SNAFU, the previous servicing system was reinstated. So much for what had seemed like 'a good idea at the time'; best of all, Ralph and Don got their old crew back.

But that wasn't the last of 30 Squadron's gremlins. As barge hunting along the north and south coasts of New Britain continued, so did losses or near losses. Just before Christmas, on a sweep between Wanamula Point and Cape Hoskins, Col Yeats and Sam Kirby went in. The accompanying crew, Don Beasely and Bruce Tiller, had seen no sign of enemy fire as Col dived at the old hulk near Cape Koas to – the others guessed – make a practice strafe. Don and Bruce then reconnoitered further along the coast; when they flew back to the hulk, there was no trace of Col and Sam.

"It wasn't Jap ack-ack, I'm convinced!" stated Bevan Wheatcroft, the Engineering Officer, after debriefing. "But I've got a niggling feeling it may have something do with the new ammo we've been getting from the Yanks." He remembered that on an earlier sortie, a pilot had been injured in the foot by what they'd assumed had been enemy ground fire. But was it that simple? Wheatcroft ordered tests to be carried out static-firing a Beau, with the armourer in charge well clear of the cockpit. Results were alarming. The man reported that every few rounds of the 20mm ammo exploded in the cannon blast tube and sent shrapnel into the cockpit! Several of the American 20mm shells were then measured and found to vary slightly in diameter. The conclusion: some cannon shells would move more slowly down the barrel than others and be hit by the following round. This caused a premature detonation and potential disaster for the pilot! Bolt immediately ordered his armourers to cease using the Yank ammo. From that time there were no recurrences of the problem – but too late for the crews who'd already bought it …

And so to Christmas on Kiriwina, 1943. Don had been looking forward to receiving the special fruitcake his mother had written to him about. He expected it would arrive via the Red Cross Comfort Fund by December 25th. Sure enough, to the Squadron's delight, a few days before Christmas letters and parcels came ashore from the supply-boat. Eagerly, Don tore the wrapping from the cake tin while Ralph looked on – then both men simply stared in disbelief as Don levered off the lid … The entire cake was thickly coated with mould – it would be pointless to even taste a morsel. Two months in the humid hold of a cargo ship had ruined Mrs Eastway's present.

Lola and Brenda's efforts, thankfully, were more successful. For Christmas lunch on the 25th there was onion soup, roast turkey with seasoning, baked potatoes and baked swedes, beans, carrots and gravy. Sweets were plum pudding and custard, fresh fruit, chocolates and lollies. Fruit cordial, liberally laced by the MO with pure alcohol, was available on every table. Except for the three Beaufighter crews flying a sweep from Cape Borgen to Lindenhaven that day, 30 Squadron celebrated Christmas in style. Perhaps it wasn't as riotous as twelve months before, at Moresby. So much had happened in the interim; too many men who'd laughed and shouted and sang at June Valley were not present to do the same at Kiriwina. Their spirits spoke eloquently to surviving comrades.

There was plenty of flying and fighting to do. January and February's Ops Board posted barge-sweep after barge-sweep for 30 Squadron – from Cape Borgen to Cape Deschamps to Montagu Harbour. Ralph and Don helped account for several enemy barges, but others sighted were so cleverly anchored under cliffs or trees that they could not be attacked. Early in January, returning from Lindenhaven they spotted a sub but it crash-dived before a strafing run could be made.

Later that month, on a sweep towards Pal Mal, Don suddenly spoke on the intercom: "Ralph – what's up? My nav table's started to shake like billy-oh."

"Yeah, I'm getting it here too. Looks like the port motor. Pressure and temp're OK. I'll see if I can get a rev drop."

A minute later he spoke again. "No joy, Don! Tried cutting one magneto, but there's no rev reduction. Synchronization's shot. The bloody motors won't harmonise. We could be in strife if this keeps up – reckon we should get home while we've got time."

Don agreed, readily, and Ralph pulled out from the Flight after a quick message to their Leader.

Their Beau shuddered like an out of sorts elephant every minute of their return to Kiriwina. Ralph got the plane down all right and reported the malfunction to his groundcrew. The men went over the port motor and soon Bert, their chief rigger, had the diagnosis for Ralph and Don.

"A good job you blokes came back. You've got five broken plugs and two U/S long leads. The thing could've packed up at any minute. These old Hercs're gettin' a bit weary, no matter how much TLC we give 'em!"

"Good Lord! Thanks, Bert," said Ralph. "I'll let you get it back in one piece as soon as you can. While you're at it, can you give the starboard motor a good going-over as well?"

"Too right, sir. She'll be right as rain in no time."

In the second month of the New Year Ralph made more entries in his second logbook: 'Barge Sweep – Brown Island to Massau; Barge Sweep – Commodore bay to Rein Bay; strike on clearing – Bangula Bay …'

Then they went to Hoskins. This was the Japanese strip on the northern coast of New Britain where Clarrie Trebilcock had bought it. It was a little east of the long arm of the Talasea Peninsula which jutted out into the Bismarck Sea. The field itself was at right angles to the coastline, with enemy aircraft approaching and taking off over the ocean. As every man knew too well, the Japanese protected Hoskins with several types of ack-ack guns. Like all defended targets it was to be given only one strafing run by each attacking aircraft before breaking off.

The Flight of three Beaufighters came in at dot feet over the forest and hills south of Hoskins, reared up one nautical mile out, then dived with all weapons firing. Ralph was low, had finished shooting and was pulling up when there was a huge CRAAACK! It seemed to fill the whole cockpit. He winced and ducked, even as he kept back-pressure on the control spectacles. Inches in front of his face, across the armour glass of his canopy, ran a wide fissure. Sweat poured down his forehead and neck as Ralph maintained his climb out, turning away from the strip. Thank God – no more noise. Every nerve in his body was going berserk.

Soon he had enough height to ease the Beau into a more shallow climb, all the while getting away from Hoskins. He assessed damage. The canopy glass was holding; there seemed to be no further splintering around the edges of the gouge. But what a shock to the system. If it had been a heavier calibre shell … Ralph's heart thudded a little faster and he increased his already tight grip on the controls. Then he spoke on the intercom.

"Just had a close one, Don. 'Dead Eye Dick's' got a mate back there at Hoskins. Gave us a souvenir of our strike!" And Ralph decribed the damage to his navigator, who whistled.

"God – you never know what's around the corner, eh, Ralph?"

"Maybe that's just as well, mate!" laughed Ralph grimly in reply. Heavens, he mused silently, if you knew the time and circumstances you'd go west, life'd be intolerable. The sonorous thrum on either side of him seemed to be in enigmatic accord.

But by the end of February, sorties were less frequent. At numerous debriefings earlier that month, crews had reported 'nil barge sightings'. The Japanese were lying very low – the Allied brass accordingly decided to conserve valuable engine and airframe time. With no big push in the offing such economy made extra sense. For Ralph and Don it was a blessed respite. They spent many pleasant hours at the north swimming beach of Kiriwina, where the water was always warm and a reef-ringed lagoon prevented sharks coming close to shore.

On one of their beach expeditions, Don learned from a fellow airman that 'Woof' Barker had pulled through after his burns surgery down south the previous year. He was back in his old squadron and eager as ever to take the war to the enemy.

" Gor blimey – wish I could say the same for myself," confided Ralph to his navigator on hearing Don's news. "I'm finding it harder and harder to work up enthusiasm for each new job. What about you, Don?"

"I've got to admit, Ralph – I'm not quite the same as I was back at Ward's a year ago. Too much bloody water – and ack-ack – under the bridge since then to say otherwise. I keep hoping the big

do'll knock the Jerries and Japs off before *we're* out for the count!"
He paused and gazed out over the placid lagoon from beneath the
coconut palm they leaned against.

"Too right. And somehow, Don, it doesn't worry me if I'm *not*
one of the blokes who marches into Tokyo. Can't help feeling
we've done our share."

"Lord, yes," said Don vehemently. "But don't forget we signed
up for the jolly duration. The RAAF decides when our tour's up –
we're in its everlovin' hands, more's the pity!"

As if to emphasise Don's point they found themselves down
for an unusual op. The Squadron was to take a Flight of aircraft
over to New Guinea to – of all things – help the Yanks brush up on
their kite recognition skills. There had been recent occurrences of
Beaufighters, Beauforts, Spits and Wirraways receiving the attention
of Yank fighter pilots or ground gunners. Too much 'friendly fire'
by over-enthusiastic US personnel. It was the reason – way back
in '42 – that the Australians in the SWPA had removed the red
from their aircraft roundels. That way the Yanks couldn't mistake
them for the Japanese hinomaru and take pot-shots at their own
side! On March 2nd, Ralph and Don were among six crews flying
across to Nadzab, staging through Goodenough. There they gave
the 5th Airforce a decent chance to see their kites. The Americans
looked, made mental notes and did not fire on any of the Beaus.
The Beaufighter men were back at Kiriwina two days later.

Here the news awaited. At last, new postings for some lucky 30
Squadron aircrew. "Whacko!" cried Ralph as he and Don perused
the board. The young pilot was to take up Staff Instructing at 1
O.T.U., East Sale; Don would head to Bankstown in Test and Ferry
Flight. It was farewell to the frontline in the SWPA for Ralph and
Don and hello to dear old Aussie.

"We've made it! *Made* it, Don!" chanted Ralph to his comrade
after they'd read the board for the third time.

"Never thought I'd see the day!" grinned the navigator. "Let's start getting our things ready and sayin' good-byes, eh?"

Within a week of their good news Ralph and Don had completed final preparations for taking a Beau south. They filled in the obligatory bits of bumph, wrote joyful letters to their families and exchanged warm cheerios with their Squadron friends. Then it was the final run from North Strip and an easy hop to Port Moresby. But Mother Nature was not about to let them go without a final reminder of what she had on offer for anyone flying in the tropics. Ralph and Don's Met forecast at Moresby was only fair – an inter-tropic front lay over the Coral Sea south of the island. "Nothing a Beau can't handle," proffered the Met Officer optimistically

Heading out from Ward's an hour later, Ralph looked at their horizon and reminded Don of the man's words. "Only a little frontal instability!" he quoted. Several miles ahead, an ugly grey-green rampart of cloud rose thousands of feet above the sea. From where they surveyed the mass, Ralph and Don could spot no way around, above or beneath it.

"Straight through – or back to Ward's?" asked Ralph.

"We've had worse," replied Don. "If I plot a track to the west, we'll eventually come out over the mainland with the wind as it is. Then we can head southeast for the coast. Won't be hard to find Townsville from there."

Ralph agreed and brought the Beau onto Don's new heading slightly west of their original track. That way the storm wouldn't push them too far out over the Coral Sea, away from land. In minutes, they were into the first thunderhead, with heavy turbulence and the odd lightning spike to keep them on their toes. The engines, God bless 'em, gave no sign of trouble.

The rain did. Their pitching and rolling machine was now in a deluge. Even if their plane had been equipped with them, wipers would have been useless – torrents flowed all around their cockpits. At times, both men felt they were riding a stormbound ship at sea rather than a flying machine. Then Ralph's top hatch began to leak. Water dripped with increasing regularity straight onto his neck. He cursed, wiping his collar and hoping desperately that none would find its way into the cockpit's electrical systems. Just dandy if the radio packed it in again, Ralph thought.

"Look on the bright side," replied Don when Ralph informed him of their new 'liquid assets'. "We've got a full fuel load and no ammo or extra weight. This bus'll keep us in the air till the cows come home, storm or no storm!"

A particularly violent gust buffeted their aircraft then and all Ralph could do in reply was grunt as he hauled on the controls. A Beau was never the easiest thing to trim at the best of times – now …

So men and machine wove their way south, doggedly and uncomfortably. But Don's plan was a good one. Somewhere near Cape York the storm began to dissipate and the buffeting lessened. "Clear sky ahead!" called Ralph with delight. Quickly, Don was able to get new bearings.

"Townsville, here we come!" he chortled to his pilot. Soon Ralph was taking them into circuit at Garbutt Field in Townsville. Refuelled, staging through Maryborough and Amberly, they finally landed at Williamtown to report and hand over their Beau. Ralph submitted his flying log to the Commander of the station. The officer was impressed with 30 Squadron's assessment of the young veteran. As pilot, pilot-navigator and in air gunnery, he'd been rated 'Above the average'. The section of his logbook headed 'Points in Flying or Airmanship Which Should Be Watched' had scrawled in it: 'Nil'. A final box, also signed by 30 Squadron's CO, recorded that 'Flying Officer Raymond is considered suitable for Test and Ferry Duties or Instructing.'

Before they parted the two companions found a quiet table in the Williamtown Mess. Over a cold and very tasty pint each man contemplated his time in the Squadron.

"What a year, eh, Don?" observed Ralph over the rim of his glass. "We've done more in twelve months than most fellows in Aussie'd go through in a lifetime!"

"Half their bloody luck, mate," replied the wiry navigator. "There're too many blokes who'll be up there till Doomsday, poor bastards."

Neither man mentioned Bill Tassicker or Bob Scott and their oppos or the scores of other men no longer flying in the Squadron. But the various figures in khaki and flying accoutrements; at dispersal; at morning or midday kai; kicking a football or bashing the daylights out of a table-tennis ball; raising a rumpus like Bill did the day he climbed the pole in the mess … they were as firmly ingrained in their recall as any of the recce photos Don had taken. So many incidents and people. Only memory would keep them alive.

Ralph lowered his glass and saw Don's ruminative expression. "And when this thing's finally over and done with – what's on the agenda for you then, Don?"

"Strike a light, Ralph. I hadn't been giving it much thought up north – what was the point? But now that you ask – unless some sprog pilot does for me first – reckon I'll be returnin' to the Gasworks in Newcastle. They'll always need tradesmen, I s'pose. How about you?"

"Well, mate, assuming a trainee doesn't write me off in circuits and bumps, I'll probably go back to Macklin's. That's the Land Agent I was with in Adelaide before I joined the RAAF, remember? Old Wilf, the boss, is a pretty decent fellow. He's always had a lot of time for me – said there'd be a spot waiting when it was all over."

"And d'you think it'll finish *this* year?" asked Don. For no one in the Allied side had any doubts about which way the tide of war was now running.

"I don't see why not, Don. The sheer number of our boys in the whole show points to that pretty clearly. God, just think of those Jap garrisons cut off in New Guinea. Hardly one barge could've got across the Vitiaz Strait to Lae in the past three months. If it's like that for the Jerries in Russia – and they're having a tough time of it by all accounts – well – our fellows'll open the Second Front in Europe and it'll be Bob's your Uncle!"

So the two men who'd flown and survived together through tropical storm and sunshine and enemy gunfire said their farewells. Both would take some leave before Don headed for Bankstown and Ralph took up his instructing at East Sale. Promising to write when the opportunity arose, they shook hands.

"Wouldn't have missed the last year for all the tea in China!" said Don, grinning. "And I'm pleased as Punch that you were up front to keep us out of strife!"

"Well – most of the time, eh, Don," laughed Ralph. "If the Squadron organises a get-together after this war's over, I'll be there with bells on. Till then, old son …"

"Safe travellin', Ralph," said Don simply.

Thus they parted, each man wondering if the course of time and Fate would ever arrange another meeting.

13

ADAM AND MAIDEN

Before beginning his instructing at Sale, Ralph was entitled to take some leave. A few days after parting with Don the Flying Officer headed once more for his family home in Adelaide. He had nearly one full month before being required again by the RAAF. Glorious!

"Good Heavens!" exclaimed his beaming mother. "You look even thinner than when we last saw you, dear!"

Ralph's admiring family had besieged the navy blue-uniformed young man on the railway station platform. He'd been kissed, hugged and generally adored – now, much embarrassed, Ralph attempted to carry his kitbag down the concourse.

"Here, Ralph – I've got a trolley!" Alf, looking three inches taller to his brother than he had the previous year, was in worshipful attendance. "Let me take your stuff," begged the boy and Ralph gladly divested himself of the RAAF equipment to let Alf bear it proudly ahead of them. Each one of the family, including Ralph, was aware of the many glances cast his way by Adelaide maidens and matrons as their little cavalcade advanced. There are a few perks in a uniform, he reflected. His thoughts may have been divined, then interrupted, by Beryl. "I bet the sheilas all hope I'm only your sister and not your girl, eh, Ralph!" she whispered teasingly.

Thus they bore their hero home to Glenelg, for tea and scones and reinduction into the genteel patterns of a city only marginally at war. The average Adelaidean would stoutly maintain that he or she knew all the latest developments in the Pacific, Europe and Africa and was – of course – 100% involved in the war effort. But like old Max, who Ralph looked forward to seeing again, they possessed only fragments of the full picture. This, Ralph considered as he tucked into a cream and apricot jam smothered scone, was perhaps as it should be. He vaguely recalled his warning to Max about the gen in the papers and the newsreels; now, with the benefit of four more months in the Squadron, he wondered if such war journalism was not for the best. Who can tell? he asked himself, for a moment only semi-aware of the laughter and chatter around him. It was tricky – awfully tricky.

The next day was well-soaked in mid-April sunshine and Ralph asked his mother if she'd like a hand in the garden. "It'll be good to feel some dinki-di soil again, Mum," he said. "Up north it's just mile after mile of coral – hard as granite and you can't grow a jolly thing."

They soon found themselves places in the vegetable patch on the warm side of the house, Ralph sporting an old pair of overalls and work shirt, Mrs Raymond in a loose cotton smock and apron. Both wore broad-brimmed straw hats against the sun.

Ralph confided to his mother his hope that the war would be over before the year was out. "Then, Mum, I'll look up Wilf Macklin and ask about going back to the firm. How would that strike you and Dad?"

"Oh that's your decision entirely, dear. But your father and I both know Wilf, and he's as honest as the day is long. Always had a soft spot for you, he has. Let's all hope and pray that the fighting *does* finish soon, eh?"

"And," said Ralph with vehemence, "maybe *this* time that it *will* be the war to end wars!" He jabbed his gardening fork into a large patch of unruly couch grass that he was gradually reducing.

"Ralph – if only …" Mrs Raymond trailed off. As a regular parishioner of St Peter's Anglican Church, she knew her Bible well. A text which had often come into her thoughts since September 1939 intruded once again: 'Ye shall hear of wars and rumours of wars …all these things must come to pass …' She straightened from her crouch over the spinach bed and returned Ralph's earnest look.

"Oh yes, son – what you and so many are going through. Things we'll never know the half of, I'm sure." Ralph gave a start. "Enduring hell on earth to end hell on earth … And yet – " She looked across the neat vegetable plot. "There are always going to be weeds in the garden, dear. Always. That's with all the best intentions and hard work in the world. And often the weeds are mixed up with the good plants and you can't tell which is which! Look at my tea roses – even the loveliest, the best ones, are thick with thorns."

Ralph didn't reply immediately, but paused to take in the tenor of his mother's words. He hadn't really thought of things that way before. At least until now he'd felt that life was improvable if not perfectible; that mankind was evolving towards some state of truth and higher knowledge and even ultimate harmony. Unlike his mother and father, Ralph had regarded religious observance more as a ritual and social addendum than as an active part of his life. Church parades at various RAAF stations and in the islands were more to be endured than enjoyed. But here was a stark insight hitting him like a 20mm shell miles from the front.

"Crikey, Mum – that's a pretty dry argument! If you're right, there doesn't seem to be much point in even trying!"

"Oh no, Ralph, that's not what I mean at all. We mustn't give up, no. I think that even if we never know our final destiny or goal we still have to go on, day by day. It seems contradictory, but *that's* the purpose and that's the direction we take in a world that so often appears to offer no direction … I firmly believe that, dear."

The woman smiled gently and the son felt a pang of envy at her calm certainty. So, even if humanity was permanently flawed, you had to persevere, find a way across or around the fissures. Just like our flight home through that inter-tropic front, Ralph conjectured to himself. Despite all the mad murk and rain, Don and I *knew* we'd make it, somehow, and we did. Can there be a hidden meaning then, some sort of guiding force we never see – aren't meant to see? It was all very deep and demanding, and – and so ruddy *impenetrable*, he mused. We just stumble on, unaware of our destination. Like flying an op without a course plotted and only knowing you've reached target when you're over it …

But such sober two-penny philosophy was laughed and quaffed away the next day down at the Pier Hotel, with Max, Ron and Fred. The friends had teed up partners for the dance that Saturday night at the Maison, and Ralph was looking forward to the occasion. Some of the local nursing sisters, WAAFs and AWAS girls would be there. High time I let my hair down, Ralph decided – what better place or company to do it in?

Apparel was the main problem, apart from the fear of making an ass of himself over largely forgotten dance steps. Most of Ralph's civvy suits just hung on his thin frame, but wearing his RAAF uniform didn't appeal to him either. Too many women collecting brass, he thought. "You'd like to meet a genuine sort or two – time for the giddy Gerts has long gone, mate," he told his reflection in the bathroom mirror as he prepared for the evening. Accordingly Ralph selected his best fitting ill-fitting dress suit, polished his black leather shoes till they sparkled and tied a perfect full-Windsor knot in the tie he'd bought for the occasion. Then it was off to the ball, driving the family Hudson.

Stepping into the commodious cheerfully lit ballroom of the

Maison de Dance, Ralph spotted his companions and their partners and strolled over to the buffet where they'd gathered.

"Who's the latest swell to hit the Bay?" quipped Max to Ralph, then began introductions. "Ralph – I'd like you to meet Emma Mathers and Charlotte Wilson. Girls, this is Ralph Raymond, the bloke I've been telling you about. Now don't go grilling him about life in the RAAF – we tried that last time he was down, and believe me, it's a sure way to kill the conversation!"

They all laughed, obligingly turning to local gossip and news for items of exchange. Nearby, with cigarettes and cups in hand, other groups and couples in service or civilian dress did the same. The five piece swing band on the small stage finished tuning and Ralph felt rapidly rising trepidation at the prospect of actually dancing. Desperately hoping he could recall the footwork required for a waltz or two-step, he wondered if a progressive dance or two might help remove cobwebs. He could handle a ten ton flying machine, knew quite a bit about complex mechanical, electrical and gunnery systems and had seen his share of violent action and danger – now, in a suburban dance hall, Ralph felt ignorant and afraid.

Emma noticed his anxiety, put down her cup of tea and coughed softly. "Ralph – perhaps you'd prefer to just watch the first dance or two and get the hang of things again. Max says you've been up in the Pacific for over a year. Golly, I'd be as nervous as all get out in your shoes. If you like, we can first try a few steps over here, to practise."

A surge of relief filled Ralph at Emma's words. She'd hit that particular nail on the head. Now he noticed her properly for the first time. A slight figure, just under medium height, with a crown of red-auburn hair fringing her delicately boned face. Her eyes were dark brown, shining and large and more than hinting of intelligence. The green satin gown and white dance slippers she wore set her features off perfectly, Ralph considered. She's attractive as well as nice – no doubt about it, he said to himself. I'll have to get to know her a bit.

Which he did. As Max, Ron, Fred and their partners took the floor for a Queen's Waltz, Ralph asked Emma about her 'life and times'. She told him that she'd been brought up in Port Pirie and had come down to do nursing at the Royal Adelaide in her late teens just before the war broke out. Then it was further training in Melbourne and in the second year of the war, qualifying as a double-certificated sister. "The midwifery's the one in real demand," she told Ralph, eyes twinkling, "with so many doctors overseas, and so few men at home to help the mothers. Not to mention washing and changing nappies!" They both chuckled, and Ralph suddenly realized that he very much looked forward to dancing with this dark-eyed girl in the green dress. Blow the practice steps!

Those cobwebs Ralph had feared simply evaporated. Emma moved lightly and naturally in his arms. Soon he was leading as moves acquired in dance classes years before flowed into his head and feet. It was wonderful. Emma felt it too. "Hey, Ralph – were you telling me fibs about no dancing in New Guinea? A girl'd think you've been putting in some serious practice!"

"Hmmm," Ralph replied, smiling into her upraised face and merry eyes, "it's all so much easier with a partner like you. I'd say *you've* been to the odd dance or two down here!" He felt a twinge of anger at the stark fact of separation that war forced on a society and envied men like Max who didn't have to go away. But then Ralph reflected that Emma was dancing with him and a whole evening of music and laughter and conversation with this beautiful woman stretched ahead.

As they danced he added, in his mental accounting: At least I'm back in Aussie, with every chance of the bloody war winding up in six months or so. He held Emma's waist more firmly and surely as they glided among the dance-floor couples. Ralph Raymond was happy; he hoped that Emma Mathers was equally so.

The following days and weeks came in bursts of further joy and mutual discovery as Ralph and Emma saw more of each other. He'd driven her home to her small flat in Goodwood after the dance and asked about taking her out again. "Oh, that'd be wonderful, Ralph," she'd murmured – and a new life for a new couple began. A football match or two, supporting the Glenelg Tigers; tea and cakes at the Quality Inn; a party with their gang. In the last sweet week of that magic month out of war, Ralph took Emma to meet his family.

"And you wouldn't credit it – 'Dinger' beat every man-jack of us!" Ralph was finishing a laughter-punctuated account of the time 'Dinger' Bell, the Squadron chess aficionado, had taken on six opponents at once in a tournament while he himself was blindfolded!

"We only found out afterwards that his mate Ron Heath had been giving signals under the table all the time!" The company's mirth increased. Then Ralph remembered that 'Dinger' had gone in off Cape Gloucester in early December. He didn't mention that.

"Now, come on everyone – eat up. There's dessert to come yet," said Mrs Raymond. "You'd be excused for thinking they didn't feed men in the RAAF, wouldn't you, Emma?"

"Well, Mrs Raymond, all I can say is that Ralph'd be crazy not to make amends while he's got the opportunity. Your roast is delicious!"

Ralph was delighted to see his family warming to Emma so well. Even Alf had been reasonably settled at the evening meal and not *too* garrulous or inquisitive towards their guest.

In the lounge room afterwards, with cups of tea on their laps, Mr and Mrs Raymond, Beryl, Ralph and Emma relaxed and chatted. Alf, nobly and uncharacteristically, had volunteered to take care of the washing up.

"That's right – we're on the run in the ward from go to whoa," Emma related in response to questions about her work in the Royal

Adelaide. "Matron Gravestock is onto us like a shot if she even suspects that anyone's not pulling her weight!" She suddenly giggled as a recollection struck her. "Heavens – I can think of poor Gladys Epps! Glad thought she'd impress Matron by collecting the false teeth from every patient on her ward and giving 'em a good scrub up. She forgot to make a note of whose were whose …! You can imagine the shemozzle – Matron was *not* amused!"

But the Raymond family was. Beryl, then working as a typist-stenographer in a local solicitor's office, laughingly said: "Gee whiz – if my boss heard about that he'd be down to the Royal Adelaide in a flash trying to drum up clients for a legal action!"

The evening rolled merrily onward. Ralph was in seventh heaven that Emma and his family had hit it off so wonderfully and so immediately. It would make the next uncertain months (oh God that it's over soon!) so much easier to take. In a few days, he was due back on flying duties. Not, thank goodness, in the shooting war, but still a long way from Emma. Amazing how life, time and proximity had suddenly become major entities for him. Each was precious; each carried so much more import than it had a month ago. Yes, Ralph Raymond was in love – for the first time in his 24 years. This was it – or rather, Emma was, and he hoped the feeling was mutual.

When Emma arranged her shift to be with the family farewelling Ralph at the station, he knew – this woman was serious about being serious. He was in a state approaching bliss. At least as blissful as one could feel on a windswept, crowded, gritty railway platform with an Australian winter approaching.

"I'll look forward to your letters, Ralph," she said as they prepared for the harsh warning note of the guard's whistle. "And you *must* write, even if – as you say – you don't much as a rule "

"Darling," (he used the intimacy sincerely, without awkwardness) "I'll be scribbling to you every minute I'm not in an aeroplane.

That's a promise. And you've got to find time between racing around hospital beds to write straight back!"

"Oh Ralph, that'll be a pleasure – but I won't put in too much stuff about the Hospital, I vow and declare!"

The whistle shrilled. Along the platform little clusters broke up as various passengers began to board the Melbourne train. Ralph said goodbye to his family. He returned Emma's frank and open gaze for a moment, then embraced her with as much of a bear hug as he could without hurting her. The engine ahead was puffing out gouts of steam, the whistle blasted again. Ralph shouted to them all: "See you when the war's over!" To Emma he quickly croaked: "'Bye, sweetheart!" and leaped onto the moving carriage.

14

THE SKY GATHERED AGAIN

The sprog in the Beaufort was finally getting the hang of a short field landing, Ralph noted with relief. He might even make the new batch of Beau crews going north soon. Funny how you missed the Squadron, Ralph thought as the young pilot next to him concentrated on taxiing their machine back to the take-off point. But hell's bells, the instructor added sardonically, distance and the old memory sure can bind on the blinkers, no doubt about it!

Then they were back at the threshold, where Ralph spotted a bevy of vehicles, shiny with duco and chrome. Hmmm, brass hats, he guessed. Wonder what they want? After making his entry in the student's logbook and climbing from the Beaufort he found out.

"Er – Raymond. Good to see you keeping the trainees on their toes. Do you have a moment?" It was the Sale CO, Wing Commander Harrington, who knew very well that his pilot *did* have a moment; after all, it was time for the stand down of morning instructors. Ralph had been looking forward to getting back to re-reading Emma's latest letter and continuing their correspondence. He'd been back at Sale a fortnight now. It seemed like six months.

The CO ushered Ralph towards the glossy staff vehicles where a group of ribbon and braid-bedecked RAAF officers waited. Salutes were exchanged and Wingco Harrington made introductions. The chief brass hat was on the Staff of none other than Air Commodore Scherger. He was straight to the point.

"Flying Officer Raymond, I've heard more than a spot of good intelligence about you. If you're the pilot it indicates you are – well – I think we just might have a job that'll interest you. Mind, it will mean a few needle jabs for the tropics again!"

Ralph's heart rate quickened. What was this? Return to New Guinea! To go back on ops – further away from Emma than ever, and …? He remembered his fond reminiscences of minutes earlier and gave a silent, inward curse. The brass hat was continuing, as if aware of Ralph's dark train of thought.

"No, it's not the SWPA this time, Raymond. We know you've done more than your share in the islands. This posting would be to South East Asia Command. You were recommended to me and the Air Board to serve as Personal Assistant to Air Vice-Marshall Cole. We need a sound all-weather pilot who knows tropical conditions and can fly twins with no fuss and bother. Do you think you're that airman?"

Ralph could only give one answer and they both knew it. If the hand from on high rested on your shoulder, however lightly, you were a fool to pretend it wasn't there.

"I – I'm honoured that you think I am, sir. I'll do my best to fit the bill."

So the formal interview with an Air Board panel went ahead. The officer-packed group conducting business was a little daunting but Ralph knew that this was really the final tick in the box. Well before this stage the RAAF had selected its man.

'Dearest Emma,' he penned late in May of 1944, 'It's with a real mix of feelings that I write. Someone in the RAAF has nabbed me for an overseas posting. It'll be a promotion as well, so this note comes to you from a brand new Flight Lewy. The rotten thing is, I'm now going to be based at SE Asia Command in Ceylon, flying a brass hat 'round the countryside. How long I'll be there is anyone's guess, worse luck. The war in Burma's heating up all the time and they want to keep it that way. But with the Jap on the run, it all points to the end of the whole damned business, and then … Oh God it'll be lovely to see you again! That last kiss on the platform – how long ago? I'm dying to hold you, dearest, and this time to *stay* with you. I can't think of a better, lovelier person to grow old with! If you want to take that as a proposal of matrimony, stage one, I'd be thrilled – but *please* say YES, my love! Am looking forward SO MUCH to making that proposal in person – call that stage two … same for our special day when (NOT IF) the war's over and done with forever …'

Ralph scrawled his feelings onto the flimsy paper for several more paragraphs. Then he read over his latest missive to Emma and signed, 'With all my love …' He wondered as he sealed the envelope if he should have mentioned SE Asia Command or Ceylon. "Oh well – the ruddy censor can deal with that. Pity the bastards have to go through *everything*, damn them!"

Soon it was time to draw his topical kit and begin the journey north – or, more accurately, northwest. He flew by C-47 to Western Australia, then over the Indian Ocean via the Cocos Islands to India. The courier pilots knew their stuff – it proved to be an uneventful trip.

Ralph landed at Bombay in mid June and immediately began preparations to meet his new CO and the machine in which he was to fly the man. The CO was his first priority,

In a large, fan-cooled room of GHQ, Ralph was introduced to Air Vice-Marshall Cole. As the RAAF grapevine had already briefed him, Ralph found the WW I Flying Corps veteran to be anything but a stuffed shirt.

"You've probably heard, Flight Lieutenant, that some of the other ranks refer to me as 'Old King' Cole! said the Vice-Marshall, his eyes twinkling. "I'm not so sure about the 'old', but I'm delighted that they see fit to employ the royal appellation. And as of now, you're chief of my pipers three! What do you think of the Expediter?"

Ralph had been thinking about the new aircraft quite a bit. He'd only had a brief glance at its manual, but he'd liked what he'd seen. The Expediter was the Beechcraft Aircraft Company's low wing monoplane, powered by twin row Pratt and Whitney Junior Wasps and with double rudders. Ralph would have a co-pilot as well as 'King' Cole to fly with, plus the odd brass hat and other passengers at various times.

Ralph said to the Vice-Marshall: "The technical data looks very impressive, sir – I'm looking forward to taking her up."

That opportunity came the next day, at the British station on the outskirts of Bombay. "She certainly looks pretty," said Ralph to Group Captain John Edwards as they approached an open hangar. A few yards ahead, ready to be rolled out, sat a sleek olive-drab and sky-blue Beechcraft Expediter. "Looks a bit like a more elegant, smaller Beau," Ralph remarked to the Grouper, assessing the business-like radials.

"Not *quite* as nippy," returned Group Captain Edwards briskly, "but I'd say she handles as well – and of course, she's fitted with first-class instruments. You'll soon get the hang of their ins and outs, no fear. And unlike a lot of the Yank multi-engined kites, she's a tail-dragger. As a Beau man you'll appreciate that, I'm sure."

Ralph certainly did. On his shakedown flight in the Expediter, he found controls pleasingly responsive and light. She climbed well, was amenable in all flight axes and had no major vices – just as he'd been briefed. Barring bad weather, mechanical problems and enemy attention, flying in the SE Asia Command might prove a cushy job. The likelihood of Japanese air attack was probably the least of his worries, he'd been informed. Now that the enemy was on the defensive all over Burma and his airforce had retreated to safer bases, Ralph's sector of the war should be relatively free of strife.

"A bigger concern may be our own ruddy fighters, the Yanks in particular," Edwards told Ralph. "Some of 'em take pot-shots at anything they see!" Ralph remembered with grim clarity his last op in New Guinea, where they flew their Beaus to Nadzab so that the Americans could pick up their aircraft recognition skills …

"But a least it's a Yank kite and a lot of the time you'll have fighter escort," continued Edwards reassuringly. "The weather, as you're probably well aware, is another kettle of fish again. The monsoonal stuff keeps us on our toes, but Met's pretty tightly organised on that score. All in all there shouldn't be too many headaches."

So began Ralph Raymond's experience of flying over India and Burma. The Expediter and its occupants travelled to a variety of airfields and Allied bases – to Jodhpur and Delhi; Bombay and Bangalore; to Ratamalana in Ceylon; to Vizigapata; to Alipore in Calcutta; Jessore, Akyab, Imphal, Hathazari, Monywa, Sadaung, Bhamo, Ledo … A host of exotic names rapidly accrued in Ralph's logbook.

At every opportunity, he wrote to Emma and devoured her replies. No earth-shattering events in Adelaide, unless one could call Nurse Epps 'shattering', laughed Emma, who hoped that Ralph was as safe as safe could be and that the Indian women were keeping their hands off her swain!

After two months in the SEAC, Ralph had settled into his job well. He began to consider himself reasonably familiar with the terrain and conditions in which they flew. 'Old King' Cole was a good stick, affable, communicative and fair-minded; at the same time he was very much attuned to his Command and its multitude of demands.

One day in early August they were at 10,000 feet between Cox's Bazaar and Akyab, on Burma's west coast. The monsoon season hadn't finished. On track ahead Ralph and his co-pilot, Flying Officer Alex Hilton, could see big pillars of cumulo-nimbus cloud reaching up into the grey heavens. Both pilots knew it was best to detour around this sort of stuff. They had no escort – the RAF and USAAF fighters were busy with other affairs that day. But they were well within Allied territory. There was no possibility of Japanese attack.

Then, total chaos. The cockpit filled with explosions, flashes and smoke – all in seconds. The Expediter shuddered and slowed as a dark shape flashed into view on their starboard beam.

"Christ – it's a Thunderbolt!" yelled Hilton, while Ralph wrestled with controls. The aircraft was yawing and losing height.

"Call him now!" Ralph yelled back. He hoped the Yank pilot was on their frequency. God help us if he isn't, Ralph thought. He saw smoke streaming from their starboard motor. The revs were going. Pressure was dropping alarmingly.

Hilton called: "Cease your attack! Cease your attack! This is Allied aircraft – repeat –*Allied aircraft!*"

Only then did Ralph have a second to think of 'King' Cole, behind them in the passenger section of the Expediter. He turned on the intercom.

"Pilot to Air Vice-Marshall. How are you, sir? Are you all right?"

"Raymond! Yes, am still in one piece. What on earth happened?"

"One of ours, sir. A mad Yank. He's broken off – for the moment. We may be in a spot of bother. Looks like starboard motor's out. I'll assess damage and send a Mayday to Akyab."

Ralph switched off the intercom and spoke to his co-pilot. "Give Akyab a Mayday. Tell 'em our position and heading. I'll do what I can to get that engine back …"

Ralph tried everything, but it was useless. The only alternative now was to feather the dead prop. That way they could still make it to Akyab on one motor. Ralph went through the procedure to turn the propeller blades into the airflow. It didn't work. Again he hit the feathering button. Nothing. The Expediter was losing height rapidly.

Ralph raced through the possibilities for them. No place in the next fifty miles to bring her down safely – just jungle and swamp. And how would the Air Vice-Marshall cope with a bale-out? Lord, it'd be touch and go for a fellow half his age, Ralph thought.

It was then that he remembered. Back in Moresby, Bob once told him how the gliding blokes at Waikerie had used the big cumulus clouds to keep their kites up on some days. The glider fliers circled under the cloud bases and gained height in the convection. If we head for the cu-nims and use 'em as stepping-stones we *might* just do it. It's worth a try, Ralph decided. He put the plan to his co-pilot. Hilton agreed.

"Our next bet is a paddy-field or swamp, eh, Ralph?" said the co-pilot. "I don't like 'King Cole's' chances in a jump, do you?"

"No fear," replied Ralph. "But here comes our first cu-nim. Keep your fingers crossed!"

And Ralph brought the Expediter under the dark grey mass of the first cloud base. Turbulence increased, but the altimeter's unwinding hand began slowing. The pointer stopped, then began reversing its direction.

"We're holding – holding …. Gaining! You beaut!' called Hilton.

Ralph called the Air Vice-Marshall to tell him what they were attempting.

"Forty miles to go, sir. We'll jump from cloud to cloud all the way. Thank God for the monsoon. It just might do the trick if our luck's in!"

It was totally unorthodox, against all their rules and natural instincts for tropical flying, but it worked. Zig-zagging across western Burma, Ralph Raymond brought their wounded machine home. The three men cheered as the Akyab perimeter came into view and they knew that it was reachable.

Hilton radioed and the field replied that a crash wagon and ambulance crew were standing by.

"Let's hope we won't need 'em!" muttered Ralph as he began their pre-landing sequence.

In the Akyab circuit Ralph monitored their engine revs, delicately juggling the throttle. He trimmed rudder and elevator as best as he could and lowered cart and flaps. Not much of a cross wind, fortunately. Turning final, Ralph could see the apron beneath their nose, wide and welcoming. He was grinning fixedly and triumphantly as they floated above the threshold of the strip, washing off height and flaring above the Akyab concrete. Bump! They were down.

"Hallelujah!" he breathed to Hilton. Then 'King' Cole was on the intercom.

"Well done, chaps! I wouldn't have thought it could be pulled off. We've certainly got something to write home about from *this* trip, eh?"

After a few rounds of very welcome drinks, Ralph did just that. Alone in his room in the Akyab Officers Quarters, he related the adventure to Emma.

" … and it's Bob Scott I have to thank for it, darling. He told me about cloud lift from his gliding days. Hate to think what could've happened if we'd had to bale out or ditch … Poor old 'King' Cole might've found it a bit much. Not to mention yours truly! Let's hope that this is the last of my little escapades in SEAC and the whole jolly war! Just another reason to be back with you, dearest. Lord, hurry the day!"

With Christmas of 1944 and the New Year well behind, the Second Front in France moved slowly but inexorably into Germany. In the Pacific, the Japanese were falling back towards their home islands – it looked that *this* year would see the war's end.

"And then," wrote Ralph joyfully, "we'll make inquiries about a church, eh, sweetest? Once the fighting's over, they *can't* keep me here for long. I'll be back to Aussie before you can say Jack Robinson …"

In May, with the Russians closing from the east in huge army groups and the Yanks, British and other Allies moving from the west, Germany was tottering. Hitler and a few of his top brass committed suicide in what was left of Berlin. The Germans surrendered. Now it was only Japan to go …

Suddenly, it was August, and the news swept the world like a blast from the God of War himself. A huge bomb – just one – had been dropped by the Americans on a little known city in Japan. A place called Hiroshima. Every building in a wide radius was flattened, thousands killed. The devastation was hard to comprehend. A few days after that, another bomb destroyed an equally unheard of town called Nagasaki. The Japanese asked for an immediate, almost unconditional surrender. World War Two was over!

Across oceans and continents, Ralph and Emma exchanged ecstatic billets doux. It seemed, Ralph wrote, that few of the British top brass in SEAC had the foggiest about the new 'atom bomb' that the Yanks had been developing in secret for years. Most pundits maintained that only a major and costly invasion of the Japanese mainland could end the war, given the bloody evidence of campaigns like the Pacific islands and Okinawa. It wasn't until much later that many realised how near to capitulation Japan had been, even without the bombs.

But now it was VJ Day and all over Australia riotous celebrations burst forth. In their hundreds of thousands, men, women and children poured into the streets of cities, towns and hamlets. Flags waved everywhere: red ensigns, union jacks, the stars and stripes; streams of bulletins flowed from newspapers and the wireless. On the silver cinema screens newsreels depicted thousands of jubilant AIF, Navy and Airforce men about to return from dozens of far away front line areas. Which were now no longer battle zones. The world could begin again.

Ralph Raymond's tour with South East Asia Command ended. The British, for the time being at least, were going to stay in India despite huge unrest on the subcontinent, but all 'colonials' were welcome to return home. This included Air Vice-Marshall Cole and his pilot. In Ralph's logbook, 'Old King' Cole made a final, concise entry: 'A very safe and reliable pilot in all weather' and signed his name. Ralph added his own signature to the flight summary of thirteen months. Their flight from Yelahanka to Bombay in the little Expediter was his last official job in the RAAF. His war was over.

15

I SANG IN MY CHAINS LIKE THE SEA

Emma was there to welcome him, together with his family. Ralph held her closely for a long time then greeted his parents and sister and brother. Along the entire platform, men and women in a variety of military and civilian garments celebrated reunions in similar ecstatic groups. The very air of the Adelaide Railway Station seemed festive, electric, more alive than ever before. It had been a long haul from Melbourne, where Ralph reported at Laverton after flying back from the West. But any journey was bearable if it brought him ultimately to Emma.

Demobbing came in due course and in the meantime it was post-war, pre-Christmas party time. Not only in normally staid Adelaide – all over the world the euphoric mood prevailed. At the same time, that broken world had to soberly begin the titanic task of renewal. Armies of displacees and refugees, freed prisoners, repatriated troops, war orphans – all needed succour and shelter. The skeletal ruins of entire cities, two of them poisoned by radiation from the deadly new monsterweapon, required clearing and rebuilding. So very much to be done. Humanity breathed more freely than it had in many years, but for a time the sweet air came laboriously.

At the Raymonds' a new life was being faced by the no longer young man who'd left his home comforts a scant five years before. Ralph made fresh contact with his old boss, Wilf Macklin. Wilf hadn't forgotten Ralph. It was soon settled – in the New Year Ralph Raymond would go back to the real estate firm on Jetty Road. After all, he had a very important future to plan and work for, a future now including a special partner.

Emma hadn't changed in the last year. Ralph found her as mirthful, self-mocking, bright and lovely as ever, and was continually thankful that he'd gone to the dance on his leave after New Guinea. They were soon officially engaged. When Christmas came they announced to their families and friends that 'the nuptials' would take place in early February.

Ralph and Emma were married in his parents' church at Glenelg, honeymooning quietly on Kangaroo Island. The couple set up home in a rented maisonette in Glenelg East, not far from Ralph's office.

Late in 1946, their first baby, a boy child they named Michael, was born. He was strong, healthy and demanding and they both doted on him. Michael grew quickly, soon graduating from all fours to using a pair of very active legs to investigate every nook and cranny of cupboard, shed and garden. Ralph and Emma despaired at ever establishing a planted area, with their robust son doing his innocent utmost to 'disestablish' any growing item!

Two years later, with conveyancy in Macklins bubbling nicely through a post-war building boom, Susan came along. She was a quiet and more delicate child, fearful of the night darkness and often teased by Michael.

The Raymonds moved to a slightly bigger flat in the same area while Ralph and Emma discussed plans towards their dream home for which they'd already purchased a block of land. Ralph's War Service Loan proved a real boon in this.

Their third child, Paul, was born in the early summer of 1949. Like Michael, he was demanding but he also possessed much of his sister's sensitivity and vulnerability. Both characteristics made him a more difficult baby to raise. One day exuberant and on top of the world, the next day he would be 'in the doldrums' as Ralph described it, going into a stubborn sulk for hours on end.

But before Paul's first birthday the world – or a large portion of it – was at war again. This time it flared on the Korean Peninsula, over squabbles between two rival states – the newly communist North and the supposedly democratic South. In actuality it was a 'proxy war' between far larger interests of the United States, Communist China and the Soviet Union. The USSR, China's uneasy ally/rival, now possessed 'the bomb'. Over three bitter years the war ground up and down the Korean Peninsula. The Menzies Government made a contribution of regular army soldiers and RAAF and RAN units, fortunately nowhere near as large as the commitment to World War Two. In July of 1953, a grudging Armistice was finally signed in Korea.

In May the next year, a previously unknown town in Indochina entered the world's lexicon – Dien Bien Phu. Here, the colonial French lost a major battle with the fiercely nationalistic Viet Minh and the next day began withdrawing forces from what soon became North Vietnam. US President Eisenhower, hero of D-Day, looked on with alarm. The French Minister-Resident of Indochina, Jean de Tourneau, had stated two years earlier: 'If the Communists win in Indochina, the whole of Southern Asia will fall like a row of dominoes.' Eisenhower believed him. Very soon, America was to begin her interference in Vietnam, and fighting intensified into which Australia would be agonisingly dragged.

That, however, was more than a decade in the future. Over this period, Ralph, Emma and their family settled into their new home at Somerton Park, the dream finally realised. Their children attended local primary school and spent much of the long summer holidays at the beach close by. Idyllic times, despite a credit squeeze and the continuation of the Cold War. Ralph and Emma were content. As the children became more independent, Emma decided to resume nursing, and was quickly snapped up by a nearby private hospital.

Ralph's father died in the early 1960s; his mother sold the Glenelg home and moved into a unit. Beryl had long since married and gone interstate with her husband to be near his work in Melbourne. Alf was making a career as a civil engineer, working overseas. Time rushed everyone on, without pause or mercy.

With all three children now at high school, Ralph found himself growing more and more concerned with events in Australia's near north. Mentions of places like Laos, Cambodia, Malaya-Malaysia, Borneo and Indonesia recurred at regular intervals in their daily papers and on radio bulletins. So many instances of nationalist unrest, government reaction, old colonial masters being ejected or threatened.

Ralph remembered the conversation he'd had with his mother in the garden during his leave. He'd said something about the Second War being the last one – *this* time, the *last* … And his dear old mum, so quietly but so convincingly giving her view that wars would always be here. As easy to stop them as to grow roses with no thorns on their stems – part of the human condition. It looked like she was spot on.

And there was also the more immediate, personal worry of Paul. Their youngest child had never quite outgrown his first mood contrasts – of heights and depths – which often came in bewildering proximity. You didn't know when Paul would go 'down', then just as quickly snap back to 'up' again. However, in his first year of high school, he joined a district sea scout troop, enjoying the outdoor life of camping, hiking and sailing. Paul seemed to be relishing the combination of freedom and discipline necessary to succeed as a scout and Ralph and Emma hoped this would give their youngest child a healthy boost on the road to maturity.

Susan, a year ahead of Paul, was making good progress at the small private secondary school her parents felt would be best for her. Michael was absorbed in preparing for his Leaving Honours exams at the nearby Whitesands High. He had hopes of being accepted for architecture at the University of Adelaide, and kept up his studies assiduously.

Then, 1965. Paul began his Leaving year at the same school from which Michael had graduated a year earlier. He still had little idea of a future career path, though he knew it could never be a job requiring strong mathematical skills. On the other hand he liked English, History and Art, in each of which he took much pride. A Vocational Guidance test that Ralph and Emma had persuaded him to take indicated teaching as a possible career choice for their youngest child.

In a wider context the New Year was even more fateful. The Menzies government was intent on seriously impressing its US ally and Sir Robert decided to contribute new soldiers to a new war. For the first time in Australian history conscripted troops would be sent beyond Australia or its mandated territories. The battleground was Vietnam. A 'lottery' system began in which, at regular intervals, numbered marbles were drawn from a barrel. It gelled to a certain grim extent with the Aussie love of a flutter – but in this case, if your birthday date came out, you won a self-loading rifle, olive-drab clothing and an overseas trip to jungle and paddy field.

Ralph read about it all with increasing anxiety and more than a little fear for his family. Michael would turn 20 in a year. But, Ralph considered, he'll cope. If his number's drawn he'll get through okay.

"It's Paul I'm worried about," Ralph confided to Emma one evening later that year as the children studied in their rooms. "Crikey, a war's nothing to write home about, I can tell you. No matter what Menzies promises about a quick and decisive result. I've heard *that* one too many times before …"

"Oh Ralph, I can see you've been thinking a lot about this, haven't you?" queried Emma gently, placing her hand on Ralph's wrist where it lay heavily upon the arm of his lounge chair. "Will you speak to the boys about it? I'm not sure that I know enough about the war – though it doesn't look as if it'll be a major one, or that it'll last long."

"That's what they said in 1914 and 1939," replied Ralph darkly. "Oh darling, how I loathe the pollies and shiny bums who use young men for their own twisted ends. There's no enemy soldier within coo-ee of this country. If we're defending it, I'll eat my ruddy hat!"

"But these communists in North Vietnam – from what I've heard they're not very nice people. Trying to take over another country …"

"It's *not* 'another country', Emma! That's the big myth the Yanks and Menzies are peddling. If truth be known, it's a civil war, one we're buying into to butter up the Americans. For God's sake, they were going to have an election for a united Vietnam about ten years ago. That got scrapped when the Yanks realised the communists would get elected by a landslide!"

"So it's not like fighting the Nazis or the Japanese in the last war?" asked Emma slowly, meeting Ralph's troubled eyes.

"Not in the faintest, as far as I can see. No matter what some of our God-botherers say about 'just wars', and 'defending democracy', this is *not* a war we should have a bar of. In my humble opinion!" Ralph smiled and squeezed Emma's hand.

Michael, independently of his father, had come to similar conclusions. In his own steady way he'd done a lot of research on Vietnam, apart from information gleaned from hopelessly inadequate newspaper reports. Before Ralph could broach the subject, his oldest child spoke one evening at their mealtime.

"Dad – about this Vietnam thing. I don't know what you'll think or say – but – but I don't think it's right what we're doing there …"

As one, Emma, Paul and Susan looked from Michael to Ralph

and back again. The boy continued, giving reasons for his views and concluded haltingly: "I don't want to fight this war, Dad. I – I'm sorry if you can't agree with me. But I won't go, even if I'm called up."

Ralph, who had long since put down his knife and fork, pushed back his chair and whistled. He patted Michael on the shoulder.

"Good for you, Mike. I'm proud of you! For months now I've been looking at the situation and working out what to say to you and Paul about it. You've been doing the same thing, obviously, and I reckon you're on the money with your views. Thank goodness you've got it off your chest … I've been meaning to bring it up with you for ages. Never had the opportunity – or maybe never had the guts to – till now. Thanks, son!"

With his architecture studies, Michael knew he'd have the option of deferring National Service if his number came up the following year. But beyond that – well, it might even mean breaking the law as it then stood. The National Service Act did not recognize an objection to a particular war. The only conscientious objection stance allowed was that of total pacifism, a rejection of all wars. And Michael wasn't sure that he could, in honesty, embrace such a bravely idealistic philosophy.

Vietnam continued. It did not, despite the confident predictions of US and Australian politicians and generals, 'de-escalate'. Quite the opposite. Seemingly monthly, more American troops deplaned at Saigon's giant Tan Son Nhut Airport. Massive B-52 multi-engined bombers flew sortie after sortie against targets in the north and later (kept secret at the time) in neutral Cambodia. Napalm, gas, toxic defoliant, helicopter gunships, tanks, artillery and a variety of automatic weapons were employed by US, Australian and South Vietnamese soldiers endeavoring to convince the North that they could not prevail. Many died, mainly civilians. But the North Vietnamese, stubbornly, kept fighting.

Michael's number did not come out of the barrel. He was

greatly relieved, while at the same time regretting that he would not have the opportunity to take a stand against the government which wanted him to become a killer.

And now, in the second year of tertiary study for the Arts Degree he'd decided to aim for, Paul was next in line for the military machine. He'd settled well at the new Flinders University south of Adelaide, blossoming in the heady freedom of campus life. Experiencing fewer of the severe mood changes of earlier, he applied for and won a Commonwealth Scholarship in his first year at Flinders. In Drama and English majors, Paul found much meat and substance and intellectual rigour. He became interested in the art and craft of film-making, soon learning skills of shooting and editing black and white 16mm film with the little Bolex clockwork driven cameras of the Drama Faculty.

Like Michael, Paul began forming strong views on the Vietnam War. He too hated it, in every aspect, and was soon taking part in campus anti-war activity. Reading, attending lectures on the war, debating passionately in the university refectory, the young man developed and honed his arguments against his government's commitment to the conflict.

It wasn't all hard yakka and politics for Paul, though. He'd kept up his scouting adventures, as well as playing for the university baseball and squash clubs. Surfing had also become a keen pursuit; on many occasions Paul would strap his board to the roof-rack of the family Holden sedan and head for the southern surf beaches. All this extra-curricular activity provided some outlet in a hectic and at times punishing schedule.

Paul read widely and beyond his subject areas, also listening to a range of music. The mournful bass tones of poet-singer Leonard Cohen; the uptempo acoustic iconoclasm of Donovan Lietch; the silver-pure soprano folksongs of Joan Baez – all made their impressions on an impressionable youth. Above all, in those changing times, the angry chords and lyrics of the young Bob Dylan demanded Paul's attention. Yes, there *were* answers 'blowin' in the wind', Paul felt, and he was going to find them …

Nineteen Sixty Nine. Paul had been offered Honours in his Arts degree, and began the third year at Flinders taking Drama and English majors. Film-making had become an all-consuming interest and early in the year the young student scripted a short movie he hoped would help focus anti-war consciousness among his fellow students. It took much time and energy – polishing the scenario, scouting locations, organising cast and crew … He also completed a radio documentary on reel to reel tape, interviewing several Adelaide citizens about their views on Vietnam. After a friend taught him some basic guitar chords, Paul wrote his first song, based on a tune of his hero Bob Dylan. This was intended to accompany the radio doco. Life gathered an urgent, seemingly unstoppable momentum.

Later that year came the crash. Paul had simply taken on too much – he could not hope to safely maintain the pace. One day in November, having rushed back to campus from a 'shoot' on a Drama film project with fellow students, Paul found himself charging along the corridor leading to his lecturer's office. He began pounding on the door. The boy was in tears, incoherent, desperate to find refuge from a storm no one but he could detect. The Drama lecturer, a no-nonsense but fair man, was in. He quickly sized up the situation, gave the disturbed student a chair and let him pour out whatever he wanted to. Could the university postpone the coming exam? Paul blurted. Was it possible to sit a practical assessment rather than a written paper? "Oh God – I don't think I'm going to make it!" he jerked out.

Then, collapsed in the chair, he asked for something to write with. When the lecturer provided materials, Paul tried to express his tangle of emotions and the agony he was experiencing. In fragments of poetry, disjointed lines, images and symbolic sketches he poured out a gamut of thoughts and feelings that to him meant the entire universe; to anyone else, sheer nonsense …

There was only one course left then. As Paul scribbled, the lecturer made several phone calls; soon a doctor from the Glenwood Psychiatric Hospital arrived at the university. He drove Paul straight to the Hospital, where the boy was placed in a ward for medication and observation. The diagnosis was a nervous breakdown. Overwork and stress, the doctor said. Paul would require a long rest, careful monitoring and medication, and – naturally – a total break from all study. He could not return to university for the remainder of the year.

In an office not far from where Paul was sleeping through a drug-induced oblivion, Ralph and Emma spoke with the doctor in charge of their son on that first day in Glenwood.

"You say it's only a minor breakdown," Emma continued after the psychiatrist had given his summary, "but what's the longer term outlook for Paul?"

"Oh, he won't need an extended recovery period," replied the doctor sanguinely. "We can be quite confident about a return to normal by the beginning of the next academic year."

"Is any permanent damage possible?" asked Ralph.

"No – fortunately there's little likelihood of that. In our experience of breakdowns due to overwork, the prognosis is usually excellent. Rest, rest and rest – if we can ensure that for Paul, everything will be shipshape in a matter of two to four weeks at the outside … Of course, we'll need to keep him under observation for the next ten days or so. After that, I'm confident there's every chance of him coming back home."

Battle fatigue, thought Ralph to himself as he and Emma drove back to Somerton that afternoon. Then he said: "You know, in a way, Paul's a casualty of war."

"What on earth do you mean?" asked Emma, a little tersely.

She was fed up with war; it had been in the news too often this last year.

"Well – the way I see it – Paul's been fighting a bloody battle in his head for the last year and a half at least. We know he feels exactly the same about Vietnam as Mike. Remember the film he showed us a while ago? Says a lot in three minutes, doesn't it? God, what's been going through his mind we can't hope to imagine. The poor kid's probably been trying to grapple with things like conscription and conscientious objection – and a war that seems to have no end in sight …. Now we wonder why he cracks up! I just wish that Mr Gorton could've been in that hospital with Paul this afternoon!" Ralph stared ahead, eyes glittering as he clenched the steering wheel and guided the car through dense traffic.

Over the next fortnight, under a strict regime of anti-depressants and tranquillizers administered daily, Paul seemed to recover. He didn't talk much to hospital staff or fellow patients at Glenwood, but then he was pretty doped up on medication. Every day he woke to the clang of the morning bell, showered and dressed and drifted down the corridor to breakfast and tablets. He helped tidy up and wash pots and pans in the annexe adjacent to the ward kitchen. Then he would sit outside near the lawn and garden area, absorbing the November warmth and thinking – at least trying to think … There was so much fuzziness in his head, and after even a short time in the sun, his skin itched terribly from the medication side effects.

What lay ahead? That was the rub, he pondered. Paul had studied *Hamlet* in his course work. Like the young Prince of Denmark, he often contemplated the choice of struggling against Fate or giving in; to 'go with the flow' as popular cliché had it, or simply go under, full stop … It was a bad trip, either way. You had to take a beating and try to get up after it. Whether in your small steps toward a Degree and demands of a career, or wading through some swamp in an Asian jungle. There were always tests, always 'slings and arrows', the boy felt. It was how well you faced them that mattered. He wondered how well he was facing them now. Jeez – he'd gone out a long way – too bloody far. Could he ever get back again?

Over this time out from the world for Paul, Ralph and Emma visited regularly. At first they found conversation with their son difficult to begin and sustain – the drugs and his inner tumble of emotions prevented any firm bridge spanning their mutually felt gulf.

Then, one Saturday late in November, Ralph was alone with Paul. Emma had an afternoon shift that day. As it was overcast, father and son sat outside, on Paul's preferred bench. With no sunshine the itching was not a problem.

Out of the blue, Paul found himself asking: "Dad – you've been in a war. Was it always clear to you what you were in it for, why you were fighting?"

Ralph was stunned. He'd not thought about his airforce days for a long time. The new war, and the possibility of Paul's inclusion in it, had become far more urgent. Ralph considered quickly, knowing that he had to reply as truly as he could. He realised that the issue must have been weighing heavily on Paul's mind.

"Hmm, Paul – that's a big question. They say every war's different, but that every war's the same …Back in 1938 – I was about your age then – I wanted to stick up for 'King and Country'. Most of us young fellows thought likewise. Hitler was up to no good, and the Empire (that's how we saw it in those days) had to be defended. I was already in the RAAF, looking at a possible posting to Europe or Africa, when the Japanese entered the war. Suddenly it was very close to home. We thought we were definitely doing the right thing up in New Guinea and the islands. On reflection, I'd say our fighting in the Pacific in World War Two was the most necessary Australia ever had to take on."

"Not like Vietnam?" asked Paul.

"No, not like this one."

"I – I've read that Vietnam is a pretty dirty war. Apart from bombs and napalm, our blokes're using torture and stuff … Did things like that ever happen in New Guinea, Dad?"

Again Ralph was caught on the hop. Things came rushing back. He remembered the conversation with Bob and Bill in the Mess after the Bismarck Sea. And he remembered, too clearly, the time of the 'clean-up'. Over 25 years ago, but it could have happened the previous day.

"Yes, Paul, I must be honest with you. We were sometimes ordered to do things we would have preferred not to do. After one big op on a Japanese convoy, our Squadron had to strafe the survivors. They couldn't shoot back. Don and I were on one of the sorties. Poor Don threw up on the way home …"

"Is that what you mean when you say all wars are the same, Dad?"

"You've got it in one, Paul. It's a lie – always has been – to claim your own side never puts a foot wrong in war. For God's sake, the damn thing's all about killing people, after all!"

"Did you or anyone in the Squadron protest to your commanding officers after that incident, Dad?"

"No – there was no point. Any man who did would have risked a court-martial. But as it was …" Ralph paused.

"What, Dad?"

"Son – I – I've never told anyone this. But now that you've brought it up … On that 'clean-up' sweep, strafing the Japanese in the water … When it was my turn to go in, I fired to miss. Made it look like I was shooting 'em, but I didn't hit one. Said my gunsight was on the blink. Of course, it didn't make a scrap of difference – the next plane got 'em. All I did was shift the burden." Ralph paused again. "I've never known whether what I did was right or wrong. And up till today, I've not been able to tell a soul."

"Not even your airforce friends?"

"Especially not them! What would they think of me, son? The 'scab' of the Bismarck Sea? A chicken …? Traitor …?"

Paul cut into Ralph's bitter self-recrimination. "Dad – I understand. At least, I think I do. You wanted to keep some part of you free of it all. A bit of your soul and spirit that – that war could never destroy … I can see why you haven't mentioned it. And I hope I'd be able to do the same if I were ever in your position … Th – thank you for sharing it with me, Dad. It means a lot."

They were on the beach. A mid-south beach of Adelaide, the father and the son. It was a week before Christmas; while Emma and Susan were shopping, Ralph had driven Paul to the surf coast on his first leave from Glenwood. Wearing a wetsuit, Paul found the irritating itching had subsided considerably.

As Paul surfed, Ralph looked along the beach to the south. Yes – it'd be about half a mile away, he calculated – those dunes – or what's left of 'em now, where we sited the guns of our battery for that open site shoot … A million years ago. Guns. Ralph thought of the book he'd been re-reading, written by a fellow who had seen a lot of war, a lot of guns. The man was Ernest Hemingway; his book, written in the 1920s, was *A Farewell to Arms.* It was clear to Ralph that Hemingway knew much about what went on in war. Even if the author hadn't seen air combat, he still understood intimately how men and women felt in a battle-zone. Ralph had memorised some sections of the novel, set on the Italian front during the First War. The bit came back about how the world (through war or any other means) kills 'the very good and very gentle and the very brave impartially …They threw you in and told you the rules and the first time they caught you off base they killed you.'

During the past weeks, Ralph had thought deeply about these words. Were 'they' all the self-righteous, ruthless men and women who had all the answers – the bullies, the greedy, the ambitious – who lived only to control, to dominate, no matter what the cost … In peace as well as in war. And during a war, Ralph knew too well, they were to be found on *all* sides, both on the front lines and at home.

As for the good and gentle, Ralph felt that people like Emma and their children – especially Paul – were only too clearly in this category. So they suffered and had to be cared for and defended by – by *me*, Ralph concluded as he pondered. If I fought for anything or anyone, he suddenly realised, it was for them. Forget about the jolly Empire and freedom and democracy and all that palaver – that's only so much rhetoric. Funny to think that I signed up with all that guff belting around my head. Only now, after it's been and gone, do I see the real gen about why I was in it. Fighting for a family I didn't yet have! And I hadn't a clue until I spoke with Paul the other week at the hospital …

Then the New Guinea days, unaccountably, came flooding back with searing intensity. For some reason, Ralph found himself retrieving memories of Lola and Brenda from the vault of years. In all that wartime crucible of masculine aggression, hatred, fear and horrible death, were these men (who didn't *want* to be men!) two of the best human beings there? For now that the past was streaming in, Ralph remembered how Lola and Brenda had visited wounded airmen in the Squadron hospital, bringing scones and cakes they'd baked especially. He recalled how devastated the two cooks had been when news of a downed aircraft had come in …

"You wouldn't read about it!" Ralph exclaimed. "Those two blokes showed us all a thing or two about how we ought to conduct ourselves. And if we can't learn – don't *want* to learn – then what hope *is* there for the whole bloody human race …?"

A shout from along the beach woke Ralph from his reverie then. It was Paul, racing up with his surfboard and grinning broadly.

"I caught some great waves, Dad!" he beamed. "And I'm not nearly as groggy as I was this time last week. Maybe things're getting better. D'you think I'll be able to come home soon?"

"Too right, Paul! You'll be back to form in no time," Ralph said.

He meant every word, and smiled quietly as his son towelled off and began packing up. Then they turned towards the cliff at the end of the long beach, and together, began the slow trek upwards.